Highland Redemption

Highland Pride,
Book 2

Highland Redemption

Highland Pride, Book 2

Lori Ann Bailey

Happy Reading!

Lori A. Bailey

Entangled Publishing, LLC
2614 South Timberline Road
Suite 105, PMB 159
Fort Collins, CO 80525
Visit our website at www.entangledpublishing.com.

Amara is an imprint of Entangled Publishing, LLC.

Edited by Robin Haseltine
Cover design by Erin Dameron-Hill
Cover art from iStock and Period Images

Manufactured in the United States of America

First Edition November 2017

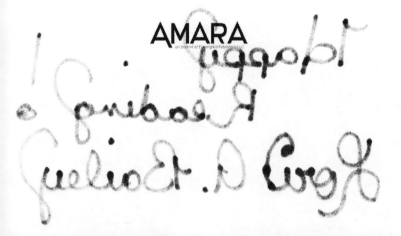

For my parents, Jo Ann and David Bailey, for teaching me respect, humility, strength, and most of all, that anything is achievable with hard work.

Chapter One

Standing in the shadows near Ross MacLean's wagon, Brodie Cameron rubbed his frozen fingers together and waited for the man to emerge from the castle. He was about to step across a line.

He was spying on a friend. But he had no choice. Ross might have violated an unspoken trust between them, and more importantly, between their clans.

Ross and his friend Neil appeared, escorting a woman he assumed was Ross's sister to the back of the wagon, but she looked as if she was arguing with them and wanted to stay at the wedding celebration. Odd. He kenned the woman, and she was not one to be forced to do anything she didnae want. Besides, when he'd asked her about Ross's activities, she'd informed him they rarely spoke, and she had no idea what her useless brother did.

He'd not been surprised to run into the feisty lass, and

fellow spy, earlier in the evening because several clans were here to plan a meeting in Edinburgh with the intention of dampening the rising tensions between the Royalists and Covenanters. His laird had sent him to see what he could discover about the upcoming summit, and it was blind luck that he'd stumbled upon Ross, the man who had been suspiciously close to Cameron lands when several cattle had recently been discovered missing.

After heaving his sister into the back of the cart, Ross turned and walked back toward the castle as Neil seated himself on the bench. The cart started forward and jolted just as the lass rose. She went down hard and could possibly be hurt.

Och. He needed to follow Neil to make sure she wasn't injured. It might jeopardize his mission, but the thought of the lass lying wounded in the back of that cold wagon galled him.

Intending to inform Neil the lass might be injured before he followed Ross inside, Brodie picked up the pace and jumped onto the wagon bench. Neil flinched, then threw a meaty fist at him, connecting with the side of his face, grazing his eye and causing it to blur as pain shot through to the back of his head. On instinct, Brodie returned with a blow of his own, connecting with the man's jowl and knocking him to the side.

With the movement, Neil pulled on the reins and forced the horses to a sudden stop, jarring the entire wagon. Grabbing onto the bench, Brodie barely managed to stay seated as his vision distorted. Neil wasn't so lucky. The MacLean man lay crumpled on the frozen ground a few feet away, seemingly unconscious.

Hearing a moan from the cart, he jumped into the back and froze. He had to squint to bring her into focus, but staring back at him was a gagged and bound woman huddled against the solid wood frame of the wagon. His senses had adjusted well to the dark of the night, but with his injured eye, he could only make out the exaggerated whites of her gaze and light colored locks. He ran a cold hand through his tousled hair. Blinking, he leaned forward to bring the lass into focus, but his eye only watered, making her blur even more.

This isnae Ross's sister.

A damsel in distress wasn't a complication he'd bargained on. When he'd watched the pair escort the woman to the wagon, he hadn't noticed anything amiss, but he hadn't looked that closely.

Why had Ross attempted to abduct a woman? He could woo any lass he wanted into bed—he had no need for force. That just reinforced Brodie's suspicions that his friend had turned traitor and was up to something nefarious.

It did appear odd, now, that they had stayed to the shadows and carried her out to dump her in the back of a wagon. Ross had only stopped long enough to give some instruction to his friend.

Decision time. Leave the woman and watch from afar, or take her somewhere safe and then find a way to salvage his assignment. If Ross wanted her bad enough to abduct her, surely he would not hesitate to use her to further whatever political game he was playing.

He glanced back over his shoulder to see the unconscious mountain starting to stir. Tearing his gaze from the man on ground, he reached out for the woman. "Come with me. I willnae let any harm come to ye."

She flinched then recoiled farther into the corner of the small space as her eyes widened even more.

Why was the daft lass afraid of him? He had just rescued her. Gently taking her shoulder, he tried to reassure her. "Ye are safe with me."

She flailed and shook her head wildly. He didn't have

time for this.

Just as that thought crossed his mind, Neil groaned. Hell, he'd had drinks with that man and seen him take out three men at once in a tavern fight.

Giving her his best dimpled grin, he tried one more time to appease her. It never failed to work on the fairer sex. "I promise, I willnae hurt ye, lass."

She stopped struggling and went rigid. If it weren't so dark, and if he could see, he would have sworn her brow crinkled. The woman couldn't be angry with him—he was saving her. The lass's reaction sent a shiver snaking down his spine, because despite the blurred vision in his stinging eye, she seemed familiar, as if he should know her. A pang of recognition flared, but he pushed it aside, because the thought caused an ache deep in his chest and he had learned to stop analyzing his emotions long ago. In his line of work, giving in to sentiment led to death.

Patience gone, he clasped both hands around her waist and yanked her up. She was thin, and he overcompensated for her weight causing her body to slam into his.

Despite her delicate frame, she had large breasts, accentuated by her arms being bound behind her back. Brodie spared a glance at Neil, who was scrambling to his feet.

Wasting no more time, he flung her over his shoulder and jumped to the ground with a jarring thud. The lass exhaled sharply as his shoulder dug into her abdomen on impact. He almost felt sorry for her, but it was her own fault for not listening. As he ran for his horse, her struggles stopped.

After easily tossing her slender body onto the steed's back, he climbed up behind her. She rocked as if she would lose her balance, but he pulled her close and held her around the waist. It steadied her, but it also kept her pinned to him while her legs dangled over the side.

"Brodie," bellowed Neil, who had gained ground, clambering toward them with his fists in the air.

Brodie peered at the dark path ahead.

"Hold on," he whispered in her ear. Tightening his grip on the lass, he dug his heels into his mount, and the echo of hooves upon hard, frozen ground cut through the silence as his horse shot through the dark.

Despite his hold on her, the movement jolted her to the side. He pulled her closer to his chest as tendrils of her long hair whipped against his face. The smell of fresh lavender teased him and reminded him of home.

It reminded him of *her*. The only lass he had ever wanted, the one who had shredded his heart. He was torn between the need to push this woman away or pull her closer.

What the hell had he done?

He could have left her in that wagon and continued his mission to spy on his friend, yet here he was, galloping into the night with a strange woman. Still, she might be the key to discovering if Ross was a traitor.

A small change in his plans, but he'd calm the terrified lass down, get the information he needed, leave her somewhere safe, then return to Stirling and finish his mission. As always, he'd turn this small distraction to his advantage. For clan and country.

He spurred his horse on.

Chapter Two

Skye's heart had clenched at the thick, all-too-familiar Highland burr of the man who'd jumped into the back of the wagon.

Nae. It couldn't be—the terror of being abducted by strangers was merely playing tricks on her.

A broad-shouldered man leaned closer, and she let go of the breath she held, because she didn't recognize the form. These shoulders were much wider and the girth was almost twice what she remembered from the man of her youth. Hoping to hide, she sank back into the depths of the cart, her entire body stiffening and her heart pounding in her chest.

But then he reached for her, and a beam of moonlight hit his face. The intruder gave her the smile that had once brought her to her knees, the one she had spent her whole childhood trying to put on his face. Now, the sight only brought her pain.

She had spent the last five years of her life trying to forget that smile, trying to shake the memory of him, trying to become a whole person again. With that one cocksure smirk, he had just shredded all of her efforts, and damn him, she wanted to reach out and feel that he was real, that this was not one of those dreams she would wake from and find him gone, leaving her alone yet again.

Many times, he'd visited her at night in her fantasies, saving her from imaginary foes and then professing his undying love, promising to never leave her side again. In the delirious haze of sleep, she always forgave him, but this didn't feel like a dream.

I'm an imbecile.

She had to remember she hated this man. He'd promised her the moon, made her dare to believe they could have the perfect life together. A home, a family, and love.

Then he had taken it all away. He had carelessly tossed her aside and left her with a gaping hole, a void that could never be filled. She had given her heart to him, and he had trampled all over it.

Her disloyal body wouldn't listen to the warning. The delight at finding herself in his arms scared her, and she cursed herself for still wanting him. Relief invaded her as he heaved her from his shoulder then tossed her on a horse.

Splayed across the horse's back, she teetered and almost lost her balance, until he climbed on behind her. Easily flipping her, he pulled her to sit then drew her back into his chest.

Damn, why were chills spreading down her spine?

He was everything she'd needed and the one thing she could never allow herself again. She still remembered every curve and sharp angle of his taut stomach and muscular arms, and the dimples of the special smile she'd once thought had been only for her—the one it seemed he now gave every lass who crossed her path.

Och, I was a fool.

How naive she had been to fall for such a heartless rake.

She would get out of this and would not allow him to break her heart again.

First, she had to figure out how she had come to be here — bound, on a horse speeding away from Stirling Castle, with Brodie Cameron holding her tight. Anxious over her future, she had fled the hall for a breath of air after an introduction to her newly betrothed, only to have two brutes grab, tie, and drag her away.

What if her abductors were Covenanters? Her uncle, Alastair MacDonald, laird to the MacDonalds would sacrifice her if the dastards intended to use her to force his clan to submit to the Covenants of the Scottish Presbyterians and turn away from King Charles and their Catholic faith.

She thought she'd been afraid of the men who had taken her, but that was before she had heard Brodie's steady purring tenor. Now, she was petrified. She'd almost rather take her chances with the others. Surely, they were less clever than Brodie, and she'd have had a much greater chance of escape.

This man who sat so calmly behind her would do much worse damage. He hadn't even realized who she was. The bastard. That was how much she had meant to him—he no longer even remembered her. She was going to claw his eyes out as soon as she could get her hands on him.

Wrists raw from the ropes, her arms ached, and the gag had pulled all the moisture from her mouth.

Why had Brodie taken her from the kidnappers? What could he possibly want with her, and why had he not untied her? What if he was in league with the kidnappers? Or did he have something else in mind? In this charged political atmosphere, with raids and murders on the rise and tensions mounting as clans took sides, it was hard to know who was friend and who was foe.

• • •

"Stop yer fidgeting, lass," Brodie ordered.

Her hands remained bound behind her back, and they were currently brushing against his cock as she struggled to free them. It made him want things he did not have time for.

Dark trees sped by as he kept the hurried pace he'd set. If he could be sure Neil wasn't right behind them, he would spare the time to stop and untie her, but with the scant light, he had to stay to the main road. The angry beast he'd thrown from the cart could be upon them at any moment.

The squirming lass threw her head back, the movement catching him off guard and sending stinging barbs through his chest. She had a hard head. She should be grateful for his interference in whatever Ross had planned for her, yet here she was, fighting him.

She flung herself back again, this time with more force.

"Stop, woman," he ground out.

She harrumphed through the gag. Then, she sat straighter and pulled away from him. He heard her take a deep breath just before she drove her hands down between his legs. The pain crippled him, and he fell onto her, sandwiching her between his body and the horse's neck. Luckily, he was somehow able to stay on his steed's back.

He must have cut off her air, because when he finally regained his composure and sat up, she started a rapid inhaling. Served her right.

It did seem to be time to have a talk with her, as they had been traveling for a couple hours, and there had been no sight of Neil. Pulling on the reins, he eased the horse to a stop.

"Ye didnae have to do that," he said as he shook his head. The throbbing ache still assailed him. Getting off the horse and walking it out seemed like a good idea.

After dismounting, he regretted losing the warmth of her body. He pulled her down, set her on her feet, and came around to her back. She tried to follow his movements, but he reached out with one hand and held her still. With the other, he retrieved the dirk he had hidden at his side then brought it up to saw at her bindings.

A small whimper escaped from her still-gagged mouth. He loosened his grip and was careful not to pull the bindings too tight while he cut her free.

Her arms fell limply to her sides, and she slowly pulled them up and started to shake them furiously in front of her. Brodie reached up to untie her gag, but her hair had become tangled in the rag, and he had to pull at the long strands to free the cloth. As it loosened, he ran his hand down her hair, fisting a handful and bringing it to his nose.

He inhaled. The smell was like a punch to his gut as he again recalled the lass who had haunted his dreams.

She turned on her heel and slapped him.

"Ye arsehole."

It didn't hurt all that much, but he was stunned. Staring at the wee lass who had just hit and cursed at him, he absently rubbed at his jaw. Unfortunately, his vision was still blurred, so he could not make out her features. She was shaking her hand as if she'd hurt herself more than him.

"Ye dinnae even ken who I am. Do ye?" the lass continued as she poked her finger into his chest as if she weren't almost half his size. The wee woman had a temper. "Take me back to my uncle right now, Brodie Cameron, before I castrate ye."

Hell, she knew him. Who the devil was she? He grabbed her shoulders before she could lash out again. Holding her and squinting with his throbbing eye, he scrutinized her face. It was dark, but recognition flared.

It couldn't be.

Blond hair glistened in the moonlight. Her pale skin glowed, but it was too dark to see the startling green gaze.

"Skye?"

Even in the inadequate light, he saw her chin tilt upwards.

"Dinnae tell me ye forgot me so easily."

It had been five years, but his body had known he held the only woman he'd ever wanted. The pain of her rejection came rushing to the surface, and he released her, backing as if burned. Hell, he had work to do, and she was the last complication he needed.

Stepping forward, she slapped him again. It still didn't hurt, but he rubbed the spot where her fingers had touched him.

"Why am I here?" She stamped her foot on the ground.

"What do ye mean?"

"Why am I no' at Stirling?" She stood, legs apart, hands fisted on her hips, foot still tapping.

"I dinnae ken yer question. I pulled ye from the back of Ross's wagon."

"Why was I in the wagon?"

He shook his head. "I dinnae ken."

"Then why were ye there to take me out?" The moon provided just enough light for him to see her eyes narrow on him.

"I am no' prepared to explain that. Why did Ross abduct ye?"

There had been a time when he could tell her everything, but she'd been gone so long he didn't know her anymore. Her uncle's clan were Royalists, or at least they were supposed to be; he'd spent years trying to determine if they were loyal to the king and his clan's religion. Even if he could trust her, though, he and his laird had decided to tell only a small few of his true assignment.

Hell, she would probably be safer if he took her back to Stirling now. But what if she could finally put to rest the questions he still had about her uncle? If he kept her close, she might reveal the MacDonald's secrets. And she might be his only link to discovering the truth of Ross's political sympathies. Either Ross or her uncle must be the traitor he'd been trying to unmask.

"I have no idea. I dinnae even ken who Ross is." She started pacing, shaking her arms out again. His gaze followed her, taking in the full curves of a woman—she'd grown without him. He wished he could see if her eyes were still the same shade of emerald, if they sparked as they once had when she'd defended him from his brothers, only now with anger at him.

Skye continued, "I did hear them say something about trading me to my uncle for something they wanted." She fisted her hands on hips that had widened only slightly but made her waist look smaller than it had at sixteen summers. "I need to get back. My uncle willnae ken what has happened to me."

"We cannae go back. They will be looking for ye." Aye, she was a complication he didn't need, but he was well and truly immune to her, so he'd have no trouble spending time with Skye until he got what he needed. And he knew all her weaknesses; surely he could charm the information out of her then return her to her uncle. She was a sore part of his past—and there was no place for her in his future.

"Well, I cannae stay here with ye."

Och, she still had a stubborn streak, but at one time, she'd trusted him. "Ye can and ye will."

Skye could be the key to keeping his clan safe.

"Ye are a treacherous rogue." She pointed her finger at him. "I wouldnae stay with ye if ye were the last man on earth." She stepped forward, invading his space, but he stood his ground. "Ye used me and tossed me aside."

What the hell was she talking about? The words cut the place inside he'd blocked off and thought long dead. Returning Skye to Stirling and forgetting he'd seen her would be the easiest thing he could do, but if he could pry the answers he needed from her, he could move on to his next mission.

"Take me back to my uncle."

Lacing the words with authority, he brought his gaze to hers. "Ye will stay with me until I ken ye are safe."

Aye, he would keep her close until he discovered why the MacLeans were after her and whether her uncle could be trusted. It was now his duty to deliver Skye safely to the MacDonald clan and to keep peace with them, but only if their laird truly was loyal to their cause. If not, he would deposit Skye with the Cameron laird and let him decide what to do with her.

Chapter Three

Damn him.

Steeling her resolve, Skye pulled back her shoulders, "Where are we?"

"A few hours out from Stirling."

"What now?"

"There is an inn not too much farther ahead. We will stay there for what little is left of the night." Did his lips just curl up at the edges?

"Well, let's go then. 'Tis cold." If there were another way out, she would take it, even if she had to bargain with the devil himself. She had better odds with Satan than with Brodie Cameron. The fallen angel would only take her soul. Brodie would take everything.

Telling herself she was not the fool she had once been, that she could keep her distance as long as she kept reminding herself he was a treacherous rogue, she prepared herself for the feel of his chest against her back when they continued on.

She inched toward the horse as he reached out to offer his hand. Hesitating briefly, she took it and barely managed not to recoil from his touch. She froze as the calluses that marred his palms brushed her fingertips. They were the same ones that had been there when he'd worked the crops and tended to the animals with her father. They were the same hands that had held hers as they'd made plans to build their own home not far from her father's, and the same ones that had caressed her more than willing naked body as they'd lain together.

How proud she'd been that he was a hard worker—she'd been so certain he would care for and protect and provide for her and the family they had planned. Once it had been all she desired. Now those dreams were dead. He'd proven to be unreliable, and she needed someone who would be around for her when tragedy struck.

Visions intruded of the day her world had fallen apart, the fear, the loneliness, and the uncertainty as fate took her father and left her with no one to count on but a family from a faraway island she barely knew. Brodie should have been there.

"'Twill no' take long to get to the inn," he said as he jumped up behind her.

"We will get some rest, and I'll find a way to get back to my uncle in the morning," she said more to reassure herself than him.

"I'll get a missive to the MacDonald tomorrow and let him ken ye are safe."

"'Tis no' necessary. I will return tomorrow." She sat up straighter to put more distance between them, but his arm remained locked firmly around her midsection, preventing her from inching forward.

"Nae, ye willnae. That was Ross and Neil MacLean who tossed ye into the back of that wagon. They are no' men to underestimate. Neil recognized me, so they will be on our trail soon. I willnae allow ye to walk right back into their hands."

Brodie's tone was clipped and stern, but one word caught and held her attention. *MacLean*. Why did she know that name?

Her thoughts turned to the authority projected in his words. He had always had a playful nature, but his tenor indicated he had hardened over the years. When Brodie set his mind to a task, there was no changing it.

Something shuffled in the woods and an owl hooted. She studied the unfamiliar dark landscape, her gaze darting from tree to tree, expecting something to fly out at them. Fighting the urge to let go of the horse and take Brodie's hands, she grabbed the folds of her skirt.

"Tis long overdue we discuss what happened between us," he said.

Her breath seized and she might have toppled off the horse if his grip hadn't increased with his resolve. She didn't want to discuss anything with him, especially not their past.

• • •

After arriving at the inn, Brodie dismounted and helped Skye do the same, then he found a tall, thin lad stretched out on a pallet in the stables and woke him. The boy grunted, but grudgingly took the horse and led it into the small space. Brodie took her hand and drew her toward the small inn. He pounded on the door until a bleary eyed man opened it, looked them up and down suspiciously, and stood back to let them enter.

Warm air washed over her as Brodie released her hand and held the door for her to enter straight into a public area with tables cleared and cleaned in preparation for the morning meal. The inn was small, and despite the pleasant temperature, the hearth on the inside was dark, indicating the fire had been banked or died out long ago. Och, it was almost time to be rising.

The exhaustion of the evening's events overwhelmed her.

"We are in need of a room," Brodie said.

"Two rooms," she clarified.

The tall, gaunt man looked back and forth between them then lingered a moment on Brodie. "Sorry, lass, we have guests, and only have one small room available." His features softened, and he looked apologetic.

"We will take it," Brodie said before she could voice the protest that was bubbling up in her throat. "'Twill save us from having to argue." One eyebrow rose as he dared her to question him.

"Ye will be sleeping on the floor, then."

"We will sort it out," he said as he took the oil lamp and key that the man offered.

Brodie passed some coins along to him. More than she thought necessary. She didn't understand what he was doing until he said, "Someone may come looking for us. He wishes the lass harm. Dinnae alert him to our presence."

The innkeeper nodded as the coins jingled in his hands. A satisfied grin passed his lips as the coins disappeared beneath his plaid.

"Up the stairs. Second door on the left. It's small, but clean."

The innkeeper yawned, and she found herself doing the same, despite thoughts of sharing a room with Brodie.

"It will do." He seized her hand and dragged her on numb legs across the room and up the stairs, acting as if she still belonged to him, as if he had the right to touch her whenever he pleased.

Her heart beat faster with each step they took. How was she going to spend the remaining hours of the night trapped in a room with him?

The door swung inward, and he twirled her around to

enter first, his large frame blocking any escape she might yet try to mount. She froze and he knocked into her, apparently not expecting her sudden stop.

The room was smaller than the storage rooms in the kitchens at her uncle's castle. One bed was pushed up against the outer wall, and an undersize table was the only other piece of furniture. There was barely room to stand, much less for Brodie to lie on the floor. He was a large man.

Either she would have to take the floor huddled up in a ball, or she would have to share the bed with him. Sighing, she closed her eyes and said a quick prayer for the strength to make it through the next few hours.

• • •

Brodie didn't even try to stop the corners of his mouth from twisting up when he saw the room and heard her gasp of surprise. Either the innkeeper had been telling the truth, and it was the last room he had, or he'd been very generous. He would have to thank the man when they left; the extra coins he had given the innkeeper weren't enough. At least in this small space he could be confidant that Skye wouldn't be able to sneak away without his notice.

His reason for keeping her so close became selfish, as he wanted answers to more than just questions of clan loyalties.

She had left him without a word and had gone with her uncle to the Isle of Skye, the island she'd been named for. Brodie had followed after her, but her uncle's men had kept him away, insisting she refused to see him. Within weeks, Skye was betrothed to another. Her uncle had schemed for a political match for her—of that he was certain. But if she'd still had feelings for him, she was headstrong enough that she would have fought for him and refused to marry another. That she had forgotten him so quickly was proof of her rejection.

Aye, she was a deceiver, and he had no qualms using her to get all the information he needed, no matter what it took.

Nudging her into the room, he stepped in behind and held the lamp up to take in the space, then set it on a small table by the bed. The door clicked as it shut behind them, and he turned to bolt it. Ross and Neil were out there somewhere.

Skye would have to take the side of the bed near the wall so she'd have to climb over him to leave—with her reluctance to stay with him, and her insistence on returning to Stirling, he didn't trust her to not flee into the night. She'd left him before when she'd claimed to love him. What would stop her now that she carried around such ill feelings toward him?

"This isnae going to work, Brodie."

"'Twill be fine. We just need rest. I promise I willnae touch ye…" He couldn't resist giving her his best wolfish grin. "Unless ye ask me to."

"Ye willnae touch me? I have heard tales of yer prowess in bed." She kept her heated glare on him as she waited for a response.

He could see how much the rumors had hurt her, but he'd never give away that his reputation as a wastrel and a rake was merely a cover. If his secrets were exposed, Argyll, the leader of the Covenanter forces, would hunt him down.

"And ye, have ye been with many, lass?"

Her cheeks reddened as she pursed her lips. There were flames dancing in her eyes. "When I give myself to someone, it means something. Too bad yer standards are no' so high."

Without really answering his question, she took the one step to drop onto the bed. After removing her shoes, she placed them at the foot of the bed and kept her gaze averted.

Stretching out, she slid, fully dressed, under the covers and turned away from him to face the wall.

He looked down at her slight form—she'd been the only thing that had come easy to him as a youth. He had been pitted against his brothers for everything else he'd ever wanted, and other than losing her, he'd done well for himself, even garnering the respect of the former Cameron Laird, the uncle who had recruited him to the Royalist cause so many years ago.

But the biggest battle was ahead, and it wasn't with his family or the Covenanters, and it wouldn't be fighting with stubborn, hard-headed Skye as he attempted to pry her uncle's secrets from her. Every minute Skye spent with him put her life in danger.

Chapter Four

Light streamed in through the window, but Skye couldn't tell what time it was. Sleep had eluded her. There was so little room on the small cot that she was afraid to move, even though the cold stung her feet and nose. In his sleep, Brodie had slung his arm over her and scooted closer, and she welcomed the warmth, but she couldn't let him inch his way back to into her life.

As of yesterday, she was promised to another.

The events of the evening before kept replaying in her head. Those memories had taken her back to the wedding celebration last night as she stood on the edge of the dance floor and watched the happy couple. Recognizing the emotions swirling in the bride's eyes as her new husband held her close and twirled her around the floor—devotion, trust, and love—she'd turned away.

Utter foolishness.

Fighting the urge to rush to the lass's side and shake reason into the girl, she'd studied the tapestry that hung on the castle wall depicting the victory of Robert the Bruce at

Bannockburn and thought of her own triumph against the demons that had held her captive for years. Sure, she would wed, but the best she could hope for in a marriage was casual indifference or maybe friendship. She'd given up on a union born of silly childish dreams and hope for the kind of love she'd seen shimmer in the depths of her parents' gazes. Her mother had been the daughter of a laird and her father a simple Cameron farmer, but they hadn't let those differences come between them. They had been each other's worlds.

Now, she was resigned to a marriage built on a foundation of Royalist unity and the blood of her kin, who were massacred by Covenanter soldiers at the orders of Sir Duncan Campbell of Auchinbreck. Alliances with other Royalist clans were becoming more important as tensions rose between those who were loyal to King Charles, and the men, like the Duke of Argyll, who supported the Presbyterian Covenants as the sole religion of Scotland.

Often, she awakened, covered in sweat, when her dreams took her to the horrors she'd heard tales of—hundreds of Catholic MacDonald women of Rathlin Island begging for their lives, and the piercing screams that must have spilled from their lips as the Covenanter soldiers of Argyll's Foot pushed them over the cliffs to the rocks and surf below.

If she could save others by forming an alliance with another clan, so be it. Despite living with the Cameron clan as a child, she owed her uncle, the MacDonald laird, and their people a debt because they had taken her in and given her a new life. At least her uncle had given her a choice of men.

Skye's gaze caught on a colorful celebratory tapestry depicting the coronation of Mary, Queen of Scots. The crowning of the ill-fated queen had taken place in this very castle. The Catholic monarch had been imprisoned and forced to give up her throne because of her religion and then hunted down by her son's own men. Skye understood betrayal, but, unlike the queen, she knew when something she wanted was not worth the fight.

"And here she is." Her uncle's voice broke into her reverie as he dipped his head to place a kiss on her cheek. "This is Collin MacPherson. Collin, 'tis my niece, the bonniest lass in all of Scotland and a mirror image of her mother."

Turning toward Collin, she tipped her chin slightly and peeked up at his intense hazel eyes. They didn't make her heart skip a beat and weren't the eyes of the man she'd once given her love to.

This man was safe. Discovering he lived in his family's castle with multiple cousins and other family members, she agreed right away to the marriage. Even if she didn't grow to care for the man, it wouldn't matter because she would never be alone again.

"Collin, dance with my bonny niece. She's quite graceful." Her uncle smacked the man, who was a good three inches shorter than him, on the back. Unprepared, the blow pushed him forward and nearly toppled him over.

Despite his reserved nature, Collin was light on his feet. "What do ye think of Stirling Castle?" she asked.

"It isnae like home. We arrived early to make preparations for the upcoming meeting in Edinburgh."

"I heard the meeting will take place in June. Will ye be going?"

"Nae, my father and oldest brother will be. My other brother will keep watch over the clan while they are gone, and I'll probably be left to settle disputes." He winked lightheartedly.

"Do ye think the Royalists and Covenanters will find a way we can live in peace?"

"Nae, but there is always hope."

They danced by the newly married couple and delighted chatter reached her ears. Nae, she would never have the bride's infatuated look in her gaze, but she would be well cared for, safe, and content to live her life with the cordial third son of a laird who wouldn't be required to produce heirs.

Breaking into her thoughts, Collin pulled her closer and said, "Dinnae sacrifice yerself if 'tis no' what ye wish. If this match is no' right for ye, we will find another way to a truce."

She swallowed, afraid that her indifference had ruined her uncle's chance for peace with Collin's clan. "Nae, 'tis fine. I would be happy to be yer wife."

"Aye, that may be so, but ye dinnae look at me with fire in yer eyes." And, she realized, he seemed quite immune to her as well.

Her mouth fell open, but nothing came out.

"We dinnae even ken each other."

Was he looking for a way out? Nae, she had to stop him. The MacPherson and her uncle would never find a peaceful solution to their feud if she jilted his son.

"Nae, I'm pleased with ye, with us."

"I'm just saying to think about it. We should at least get to ken each other a little better. I'll ask for time to come court ye on yer uncle's island."

Only a short while later, Ross and Neil MacLean were stuffing her in the back of a wagon and destroying her hopes of a peaceful future. What would her uncle and Collin do when they discovered her missing? Would her chance to broker peace between the clans be destroyed?

As she considered her options, she burrowed under the covers.

• • •

Waking on her back with Brodie's gaze meeting hers, her heart skipped a beat.

"Were ye watching me sleep?"

"Aye, I was." A lazy smile coupled with his husky voice followed. "I never got to wake to find ye next to me."

Sitting up quickly, she threw the blankets at him and scooted off the end of the bed while changing the subject. "I'm hungry."

"I am, as well," he burred with a suggestive tone.

She ignored him, and he must have received the message, because the bed shifted as he rose to pull on his own shoes. Making the mistake of turning around, she froze at the image before her.

Brodie's bare ass, lean and sculpted, looked hard as oak, but smooth and velvety at the same time, and her hand itched to close the short distance and caress the rounded globes to test the contradiction. He stretched and her eyes were drawn up the slight incline to his tapered waist, then farther to the wide expanse of his sinewy shoulders. Blood heating, she struggled with the desire that woke from some forbidden place inside her.

He had changed over the years, and now, in the morning's light, he was even more bonny than he had been as a youth. When he turned, she gasped at the unmistakable evidence that his thoughts had strayed in the same direction as hers. His gaze dropped from her eyes to her lips and down to her still-clothed body.

She blinked and remembered she was newly betrothed and shouldn't be looking at a man other than her husband. Snapping her eyes closed, she tried to visualize Collin MacPherson's face and turn her thoughts to him, but the only features she could recall were those of the man she wanted to forget. Her lids flew open.

Giving her a wolfish grin, he tilted his head sideways in a flirtatious expression that made her want to forget the hell he'd put her through. She couldn't help it—her mouth went dry. Or was it watering? Either way, she gulped and tried to control her racing heart. She turned her head, but it was too late. The image of his well-sculpted form was burned into her memory. His massive shoulders, taut stomach, and fully erect penis would haunt her the rest of the day. Clearing her throat, she stood and walked for the door.

"Ye are the devil," she muttered without turning back toward him and reached for the door.

"Hold on. Ye cannae go without me. What if Ross and Neil are here?"

She kept her fingers curved around the handle, but did not look; the *whoosh* of his plaid as he threw it over his shoulders brought some relief from the torment. The bed squeaked, and she was certain that he was pulling on his boots and would be decent, but she decided not to risk a glance.

Another whine sounded from the bed as it protested the loss of his fine form, and gooseflesh rose on her skin as she felt the air part for him when he came up behind her. Lifting the latch and moving to open the door, she tried to flee the room, but he put his hand on her arm. She caught her breath at the light touch and looked around.

Shaking his head, he motioned for her to step back into the small chamber, and she did. He cracked the door silently and stuck his head out, peering in both directions. After pulling the door in, he said, "'Tis clear."

He led the way down the stairs, but as they neared the bottom he held out a hand to stop her advance. Realizing he really was concerned the men who had abducted her would follow them, she stilled and prayed he was wrong. His head turned to scan the room for threats, then he motioned for her to continue.

As they took a table in the empty room for a meal, a relative calm washed over her at the prospect of quenching the pain in her empty belly. Either the guests in those filled rooms had left earlier in the morning, which was likely, considering it was time for the midday meal, or there had been no others.

She was helpless to protest when the innkeeper's attractive, rosy cheeked daughter started ogling and openly flirting with Brodie. He seemed not to notice or care, but it burned her inside that women threw themselves at him all the time.

When the buxom wench served him a handsome portion of eggs, the harlot bent low enough to reveal the milky expanse of her nearly exposed chest. Skye glanced down to lament that her own breasts were quite small in comparison, then ground her teeth and clenched her fists under the table. If the girl dipped any farther, she might fall out of her gown. To add to the insult, when the girl straightened, the cheeky lass didn't even offer her any food, just plopping the rest in the middle of the table for her to fill her own trencher.

To be fair, Brodie didn't encourage the woman, but she could only assume his reputation preceded him, so she blamed him anyway. Tapping her foot a few times, she tried to fight the jealousy, but it irked her. What made it worse was, she shouldn't care. She no longer had a claim to him; even more, she did not want one. But some irrational part of her said if she could not have him, no one should.

"How long will it take us to get back to Stirling?" She drummed her fingers on the table and turned her eyes from the full-figured lass lurking in the corner, waiting to service any need Brodie had.

"Nae, I am taking ye to Kentillie."

Her fingers froze. "Surely, ye can have any lass ye want. Why saddle yerself with one who doesnae want ye?"

Something she didn't recognize flashed in his eyes. "Ye are the only lass I ever wanted," he countered.

"From what I hear, ye want every lass in Scotland." She could hear the bitterness in her tone.

"Were ye keeping tabs on me then, sweet?" His body leaned in closer to hers. Finding it hard to breathe, she slid her chair back from the table.

One side of his lip curled up in a wicked grin. He could see she was jealous, damn him. The dimple on that side appeared, and her heart skipped a beat. No man had the right to be so appealing, and it galled her that she still fell for his charms.

"Dinnae call me that, rogue," she snapped.

He leaned back lazily. "How is it ye ken so much about me, but I havenae heard what ye have been about these last few years?"

"I am a private person. I dinnae wish for my dalliances to be on display for all of Scotland." Balling her fists, she remembered the string of events that had changed her life. She had sought out Brodie to tell him her father's illness had worsened, and that she didn't want to be alone. She was sure he would come sit with her while she nursed her father back to health. Not finding him at his house, she darted toward his stables and saw more than she wished to see.

He was there. So was Nora Stewart. Brodie moved in like he was going to kiss her, but then pulled back, laughing. Her heart, already devastated by the declining health of her only family on Cameron lands, split beyond repair. Then, Brodie went down on his knee in front of Nora, and her carefully crafted world fell into ruins.

Anger burned in the pit of her stomach. Her repeated requests for him to tell her where he'd vanished had only been met with half-truths and evasion. But now she knew why—he'd been with some harlot.

She had been days away from her eighteenth birthday and had given Brodie Cameron her heart and soul. Only two weeks before, she had given him her body. He had told her everything she'd always wanted to hear, that they would marry, have a large family, and live happily ever after.

Returning home and pushing aside her misgivings to focus on tending to her only parent, she vowed to confront Brodie once her father was better. But Brodie didn't show up that night for the late meal like he usually did, or the next day when her world had fallen apart.

She'd been all alone with her father when he'd died. She had needed Brodie to wrap his strong arms around her and let her know she would survive and she shouldn't be afraid of being on her own because he'd always be there. But he hadn't been. Not able to go for help, she'd spent the whole night with her father growing colder.

She vowed she would never be alone and helpless again.

Brodie had not even attended the funeral. Although she hadn't planned to leave, she'd not argued when her uncle had come and taken her to his home on the Isle of Skye before Brodie even bothered to return.

Dropping the fork, she wiped at her eyes with the sleeves of the same olive-colored gown she'd been wearing since the wedding. After jumping up, she headed for the outside before he could see how affected she still was by his betrayal and indifference. She ran for the door, but he was right behind her, catching her and spinning her to face his dark gaze before she made it through the door.

Anger blazed in his eyes. "Until we find out why the MacLeans tried to kidnap ye, ye best keep yer head about ye, Skye, and no' be running off. 'Tis no' safe."

Chapter Five

Brodie was gathering his pack when his gaze drifted to the south-facing window as movement caught his attention. Riders approached. Squinting, he made out a wagon and a man on horseback beside it, but they were still some distance away.

Hell, it was Ross and Neil, although he'd done all he could to cover their tracks last night. His jaw started to tic, because these men had put their filthy hands on Skye. He dashed toward the hall to get Skye to safety before they found her.

Relieved to see she hadn't gone far—she held a large basket in one hand and was laughing with the innkeeper—Brodie pulled out a handful of coins and tossed them to the man. Some clinked to the floor, missing the outstretched hand of their host, and the man stooped to retrieve them. "Men approach. Keep them busy and dinnae mention we were here," he muttered to the innkeeper.

"Aye. I will stall them. We appreciate yer patronage," the man reassured him.

He clamped onto Skye's empty hand and pulled her

toward the back. She must have recognized his urgency, because she didn't argue or pull away.

The stables were thankfully on the north end of the property.

Mounting the horse quickly, they were off and probably out of sight before the blackguards had reached the inn. He kept looking over his shoulder, but there was no pursuit and no sign that the men realized how close they were to catching up to them.

"We should be going back to Stirling." Skye protested only a few moments after they'd left the inn, and he was reminded how stubborn and strong-willed she could be. Her tenacity had seen him through some of the tougher times with his family during his youth.

"Ye ken that isnae a good idea." Certainly, they could double back and head for Stirling instead of Kentillie, but there were three problems with that.

First, he'd never discover why Skye had left him or what hand her uncle played in taking her away right after her father's death. Second, he didn't fully understand the threat against her. If the MacLeans were after her, who else might be waiting to do her harm, and what did it have to do with the ongoing conflicts in the region?

Which brought him to third—he had a prearranged meeting today to discuss a recent spate of activity amongst the Covenanter crusaders in the area with the second in command of the Royalist Resistance—none other than Ross's sister, Isobel MacLean. Maybe while he was there, he could discover what her brother was up to.

"This Neil called yer name. He kens who ye are, then?" she asked.

"Aye. He does."

"Does he ken where ye live?"

She had a valid point, but back at home, he knew the

terrain and could better protect her.

"He kens I live on Cameron lands, but no' where. I am sure if he tries hard enough he will find it. But better to face Ross and Neil on familiar ground than somewhere I cannae properly defend ye. Anyway, when we get back, we can let Lachlan ken what is going on."

He smiled as he thought of his cousin Lachlan and his new wife, Maggie Murray. She would love Skye and would welcome her with open arms, not to mention all the other lasses with whom she had been friends as a child. If the Cameron women made her feel welcome, she might never want to leave.

Knowing she'd have the protection of the entire Cameron clan, Brodie could return to days filled with delivering covert messages to dangerous people and nights hiding in the shadows, playing a game of politics that would one day destroy him and anyone he loved. Every day in this business, the risk his identity would be discovered grew, and if it were ever uncovered, Skye's mere presence in the room with him put her life in danger.

An image of Donald MacKay's battered and bloody wife swaying in the wind from a tree in the spy's own yard reminded him of what was at stake.

Suddenly, it was Skye's face he saw on the swinging figure, and bile rose from his gut. He would never risk exposing her to his secret life or chance letting Argyll get his hands on her.

• • •

Brodie eased up slightly on the steed but kept a steady pace. Skye began to relax, and her curves sank into him as she fell into a peaceful sleep. He inhaled her lavender scent and let his thoughts stray to a place he couldn't afford.

The mystery of what had happened between them still

eluded him. Surely she kenned how much her father had meant to him, and he'd been destroyed when he'd returned home to find them both gone. A last minute, urgent, covert mission in Inverness had kept him away longer than intended. Wanting to assure her he would take care of her, he'd rushed to her uncle's castle, only to be turned away, beaten nearly to death, and told Skye never wanted to see him again.

Throwing himself into his work eased the sting of the rejection and kept him from going mad. He was now so deeply embedded in his secret world, there was no possibility of ever getting out with his life, much less exposing her to it.

He scanned the barren, dormant trees amongst the still green pines and frozen dirt as they made their way west instead of north. Hoping Skye wouldn't be familiar enough with the roads to know they weren't headed straight to Cameron lands, he debated what to do with her while he met with Isobel this evening.

Skye stirred in his arms. "'Tis so cold," she said as she nuzzled into him. "Do ye remember that winter it was so cold, and Father was out late? Ye came over and we tried to start the fire in the hearth." Her teeth chattered, but despite that he could hear the mirth in her voice.

He laughed. "Aye, I do. Ye threw all the cooking grease in the hearth. The flames were shooting up almost to the ceiling."

"Then ye tossed the water on it." Her lilting glee rolled over him, warming him like the summer sun.

"I ken better now." Her laughter died, but she seemed more at ease.

"Aye, me as well." He shook his head. "Yer father tanned my hide that night. He told me to never put ye in danger again. He said I was responsible for taking care of ye."

After that evening, Skye's wellbeing had become his priority. But he was young, and self-doubt, the feeling that he would never be good enough for her, had taken hold—until the Cameron laird had taken him into his confidence and given Brodie a position he thought would make him worthy of her. By then, it was too late.

He straightened his shoulders and tilted up his chin, urging the horse forward again.

The day Brodie overheard what her uncle said about him played in his head—that was the day he'd started his quest to uncover the truth about the MacDonald laird's loyalties. The day he'd discovered what the Royalist Resistance was up to and how, despite their ruthlessness, they could be used as a source of information in order to protect the clan.

The skies had been clear and the weather unusually warm for an early June day when he'd made his way to Skye's house to share the late day meal with her and her father. Raised voices reached his ears, drawing his attention to the open windows. As he continued to approach, the argument intensified, and he heard his name mentioned.

He flattened his body to the cool stone of the house next to the window, far enough away he wouldn't be noticed.

"Ye cannae mean to let her marry that farmer."

Brodie lurched at the raised, unfamiliar voice and the implications.

"Aye, I do. He will make her happy." Skye's father, Darach, defended Brodie, and he was able to take in a shallow breath.

"Like ye did for my sister. Ye never should have brought her here," the imperious tone shot back, and it dawned on Brodie who the man was: the MacDonald. Skye's uncle.

Silence dragged on.

"We had a good life, and she was happy." The hitch in Darach's voice called to his heart.

"Ye ken she could have married a laird and never wanted for anything. Instead, she ended up here, when she could have been cared for in a castle around family. Ye willnae do the same to her daughter."

Nae. Skye had always been Brodie's; they couldn't take her away from him. His jaw clenched.

"She will marry who she wishes," Darach insisted, still calm and controlled.

"Ye ken John Macnab would be a good match for her. He'll be laird one day."

"And what of the Macnabs? Do ye ken they havennae stood for the king and their religion? Seems to me the Macnab laird chooses the side that fits him." A dry sarcastic tone stole into Darach's words.

The life he'd always envisioned for Skye and him suddenly seemed in jeopardy. He fisted his hands in his plaid, ignoring the sweat that dripped and stung the back of his neck. Darach wouldn't let his deceased wife's brother tell him what to do, but the man was the MacDonald laird. Would he seek out the Cameron and force Skye's father to acquiesce?

"Macnab is a sensible man," came the dry reply.

"Nae, I willnae allow it. She loves Brodie. He'll keep her safe and comfortable. 'Tis what she wants."

"Aye, but sometimes what we want has to be given up for the good of all."

"No' in her case. Yer sister wouldnae have wanted it, and ye ken it."

Movement caught his gaze and pulled his attention from the heated exchange as Skye approached along the trail from Kentillie, the Cameron stronghold. The conversation became a blur as his thoughts scattered.

The next words that registered shocked him to his core, "So, ye will send her away and side with the Covenanters, then?" Never having heard Darach speak in other than a contented tone, the venom in his voice stiffened Brodie's spine.

Skye hadn't noticed him yet, but she would soon.

Knowing he couldn't face the MacDonald laird at the dinner table, Brodie skirted around the cottage before she got closer and carried the news of the MacDonald's possible sympathies with the Covenanters directly to the Cameron laird. After discussing the matter with his uncle, Brodie found himself at a local tavern. While there, for the first time in his life, he found himself drunk and spilling his guts about Skye's uncle to the first listening ear.

It just happened to be to the one man who was interested— Alexander Gordon, who was mounting a resistance against the Covenanters currently terrorizing the Highlanders who wanted nothing more than to keep their own religion. In one evening, Brodie had become a spy for the Cameron clan and met the leader of the Royalist Resistance, who was the most valuable source of information in Scotland.

Now, as they trotted toward the tavern where he'd planned to meet Isobel, second in command of the Royalist Resistance, he thought about how far he'd come. No longer the simple farmer who had wanted a life filled with family and love, he was now a hardened Royalist whose only loyalty was to his God and his clan.

Chapter Six

After they'd stopped at another inn for the evening, Skye peeked across the plate of stewed meat, roasted potatoes, and bread that sat on the small table between her and Brodie. While she nibbled at a bite of soft, buttery loaf, savoring how the morsel melted in her mouth, she marveled at how he looked so different, but still the same.

His thick dark hair was windswept from riding all day, but at the same time it was appealing on him. Och, everything was attractive on him, even the twin dimples that weren't showing at the moment. While his attention was diverted by the food, she took in his golden cheeks and the long lashes framing those chocolate eyes that reminded her of warm summer nights and home. Eyes she'd never expected to see again.

Her thoughts turned to another Highlander who promised her a home and family and security. The man across from her had promised those things once, but then took it all away.

What would happen when Collin MacPherson discovered she'd spent two evenings in a room with Brodie? Would it jeopardize the union her uncle had made for her?

Blaming him for the possibility her betrothal might be ruined, she stabbed a small potato piece, met his gaze straight on, and asked, "Will ye send word to my uncle to come get me?" Stuffing the morsel in her mouth, she chewed the tender bit and held back the curses she wanted to fling at him for ruining her future.

"Aye, I will make sure 'tis done tonight."

Unbidden, her thoughts went to spending another night alone with him, and her face tingled with embarrassment. His dark gaze turned to hers and seemed to take in more than what she wanted to reveal.

She scooped up another bite then turned away, hoping that he hadn't guessed her heart still fluttered when his gaze landed upon her.

"Does yer uncle side with the Covenanters?"

Blinking at the unexpected question and the strained tension in his voice, she said, "What? Are ye insane? Why would ye think such a thing?"

"Has yer uncle had any dealings recently with any of the Royalist clans?"

Something in the depths of his eyes told her he wasn't jesting. He seemed dangerous, not the playful lad of her youth, but rather a fierce Highlander hardened by battle, politics, and divided loyalties.

"Nae, and even if he did, why would I tell ye?" She felt an urge to defend her uncle, who had given her a family when she'd lost everything.

Brodie's eyes clouded, taking on a deeper hue and pinning her with distrust. After a swig of ale, he pounded the cup on the table, causing her to flinch. He pushed back. The wooden chair creaked and let off a jarring screech. He rose and walked for the door. "Bolt the door and dinnae leave the room."

She stood up. "Where are ye going?"

"I'm going to write to yer uncle. 'Tis safer if ye stay here." He didn't turn to face her, but his voice no longer held the anger it had moments earlier.

"Ye dinnae mean to leave me alone in here?"

"I willnae be far."

They were in a village she'd never seen, and she had no coin and no way to get home. Would he come back for her this time? *Och*, she hated to be alone, even if that currently meant spending the time in a room with Brodie Cameron.

He pulled open the door, walked through, and shut it without saying another word.

Skye paced the open space between two beds in opposite corners of the room. Trying to keep panic at bay, she shuffled toward the window and the dying light of the day. She glanced out just in time to see Brodie strolling across the street and several doors down to a large building with a sign that read, *The Gray Goose.*

A tavern. That scoundrel. He was going out drinking while she sat like an obedient child waiting for him to return. How could she trust a man who would so easily mislead her?

Raw anger stung her cheeks and ate at her. He left her so that he could have a drink. Och, she would have let him drink in the room, or he could have taken her with him. Sinking onto the bed, she rolled the options around. She couldn't flee, because she had no way to get back to Stirling. But, she could go to the innkeeper and insist he send for her uncle and let him know she was here against her will.

Or better—it was time to confront the arse.

Straightening her shoulders, she rose and marched toward the door. She was going to let Brodie Cameron know exactly what she had gone through when he had been off in the pubs while her father died.

She was down the stairs, across the street, and at the door

of the Gray Goose before she could question what she was doing.

When the door swung open, she froze. Holding on to the frame to steady herself, she watched as Brodie, arm around a lovely lass with hair so light brown it appeared gold, leaned in as if he were telling her secrets and inviting her back to their room. He hadn't come down to get a drink, he'd come to find a wench with more curves than she had to whet his appetite.

The bonny lass caught her eye, and as her full lips moved, Brodie turned to see her in the door. A flash of anger sparked in his gaze, but then was gone, and he turned back to the woman at the table and offered her a grin.

Skye turned, bumping into a man whose arms circled her waist and pulled her to him. His rat-like gaze looked hungry. "Come on now, lass. I'll take care of ye."

Luckily, she was able to back away and pull free from the hands that felt like greedy talons grasping for a meal. If she had coin, she would go somewhere else, but she had nothing save the clothes she wore, so she ran back for the inn, stumbling up the stairs, then finally slamming the door and bolting it behind her.

• • •

Why hadn't she listened and stayed in the room? Aye, she was headstrong, but he'd warned her of the danger she was in. Brodie cursed, knowing he couldn't go after her and chance jeopardizing his mission or compromising his identity.

With feigned drunkenness, he called over to one of the serving lads and dropped a coin in his palm, "Follow my wife back to the inn and make sure she's bolted the door. She cannae abide my interest in other women." The lad snorted in commiseration. His fingers curling around the payment, the boy hurried out of the tavern, returning quickly with a short nod.

Assured Skye was again safe, Brodie let out a breath and returned his attention to Isobel. The spy hadn't moved, her back to the wall at a table that afforded her a view of the whole room. Motioning to a young lass, he held his hand up to indicate he'd like another ale.

A man approached the table, eyeing Isobel as if he were looking for a little bed sport. Before the lout said a word, she pulled a dirk from the depths of her skirts and slammed it on the table between them, not letting her hand move from the hilt or her steely stare leave the unwanted guest. Silence filled the room and the man gulped, backing away, nearly running over Brodie in his haste to escape. The man had good cause to be scared of her—Isobel wouldn't hesitate to kill.

It was one of the things that worried him about her—she was drawing too much attention to herself and would be outed if she kept it up. Meeting her here had probably been a mistake, putting them both at risk. He'd have to talk to Alex Gordon about finding a way to get her to abandon whatever asinine quest had brought her to this point in the Royalist Resistance.

Scooting his seat closer to hers and leaving his exposed back to the room, he leaned the chair onto its hind legs and cheered loud enough for the whole place to hear, "Showed him, ye did, lass." Then he let out a raucous laugh that was harder to produce than usual, his lungs still tight over both what Skye had seen and his new concern for Isobel.

The barmaid hurried to his side with a new cup. Trailing her hand across his arm, she purred, "Just yell out for me if ye need anything." He'd given her enough coin for three ales earlier, but he didn't think money was what the lass wanted as she winked at him.

Turning his attention back to the table in front of him, he picked up the cup and pretended to drink. "The meeting is set for June in Edinburgh."

"Will Argyll be there?" Isobel eased, pulling the dirk back. It disappeared beneath the table.

"My guess is yes, but I amnae certain yet. I do ken 'tis a trap for the Royalist lairds, though. I just havenae figured out who is behind the plot."

"I'll look into it."

"What's Ross up to?"

Rolling her eyes, she said, "I've told ye I dinnae keep track of him. Unlike ye, he really does appear to be useless."

"I need to ken what he's been doing."

Shrugging off his concern, Isobel asked, "Who is the wench? She's no' yer wife."

Looking down into his cup, he hid his lips as he murmured, "Dinnae worry with her. Do ye have any news?"

"Aye. Something's upset Argyll. He sent riders out all over the Highlands this morning." She hid her mouth behind her hand as she spoke.

"Why?"

"I tracked down one of them. The man said he was after some lass. The earl wanted her bad enough to offer a hefty reward for her capture and a smaller one for proof of her death."

If Earl of Argyll wanted this woman dead or alive, she would be better off dead. "Hell. What did the woman do?"

"No one kens, and the man I stopped needed persuading"—exposing her hand, she flashed her dirk then returned it to her lap—"to tell me who she was. Argyll doesnae want what happens to her associated with his name."

"Who is she? Mayhap she kens something that will help us. Does Alex ken where to find her?" This time he took a sip of the ale to wash down the worry and anticipation. Maybe this was their chance to stop the Covenanters.

"The MacDonald of Skye's niece. She's named after the

island, which confused me at first, but it makes sense now." Isobel let out a little laugh like she was amused, but it barely registered with Brodie as every part of him froze and time ceased to move.

The fingers around his cup went numb.

Nae. She couldn't be talking about his Skye. What would Argyll want with her? Had her uncle gone back on some deal he'd made with the Covenanter leader?

"Do ye ken her?" Isobel asked.

Forget the serving lad's assurance. He had to get back to the room to know Skye was still there and to keep her safe.

"Have Alex meet me. The Healthy Hen. In five days." He was calculating how long it would take him to get back to Kentillie and then to enlist Lachlan in hiding Skye and protecting her from whatever was going on. Pushing back from the table, he knocked his chair to the floor.

"Why? 'Tis much sooner than yer usual meeting."

"Because the lass who followed me in here tonight was Skye MacDonald."

He was stumbling toward the door when he heard Isobel's reply, "Oh, damn!"

Och, the woman had to be more discreet, and she needed to get out of this business before Argyll found her.

The shroud of night outside wrapped around him, and he was reminded how early the darkness crept in on a Highland winter night. It had been a warmer day, almost pleasant, but now a bone deep chill indicated another shift in the weather.

After using his key to peek into the room, assuring himself Skye was there, he strode back down to the innkeeper's study, where he spent the next hour, his eye on the stairs, composing two letters to the MacDonald—one as Brodie, to let him know she was safe in his care, then another in different handwriting as the Raven to pass on the information that Argyll was after his niece.

Pulling the seal from the hidden pocket in his plaid, he used the red wax on the desk to close the letter and stamp it with the signature R of the Raven. Then, he took the one from his sporran with the letters BC on top of the Cameron badge and stamped the other with a brownish wax he had found.

Afterward, he tracked down the post-boy from the town, who had been approved for contact by the Royalist Resistance, and deposited the envelope from the Raven into his care. He held on to the other one to send from an alternate location.

Back in the night air, the wind slapped him with a frenzied fury. A storm he couldn't stop brewed and bubbled.

The first priority was getting Skye to a safe location and then discover what she had to do with Argyll and the Covenanters.

. . .

They rode most of the next day in silence, the ground still wet from last night's fast moving storm and the lingering mist in the air. Skye had said little to him when he'd returned from his meeting with Isobel, and was evasive and still angry with him, but that was all right because he was still trying to decide how to broach the subject of Argyll and her uncle. All the while, he attempted to puzzle out why Ross would have gone after Skye even before Argyll had sent out the orders that put her life in jeopardy.

What if Ross had been Argyll's first attempt to get at Skye and had failed? The earl may have sent out others. Yet, Brodie was finding it hard to believe the MacLean man would work for the Covenanter leader.

The sun was low in the sky, and he decided it was past time to stop for a meal, but he'd been so anxious to put distance between them and the threat of exposure, that he'd not stopped to consider Skye's needs.

Ross was probably ahead of them, traveling straight toward Cameron lands, or on his way back to MacLean lands. Since they'd taken the detour east, his old friend had most likely continued on what should have been their course, and probably had no clue as to where they were.

The barren, open field they came upon seemed an adequate spot to stop. If they sat in the back corner, he would have a good view of the road without travelers being able to see them. After guiding the horse to the area he had in mind, he dismounted then helped Skye down. She didn't balk and turn away, only appeared resigned to spending the time with him.

Laying an extra plaid down on the soft clumps of wet, brown grass, he eyed the path they just came from, as Skye sat and unpacked the basket the innkeeper's wife had filled this morning.

"Good, 'tis fresh," she said. "I was worried after what they'd served this morning."

He sat next to her, so close they almost touched. She bristled, and he thought he saw her fingers tremble, but he turned so as to not call attention to her uneasiness—and because he wanted to pretend her mistrust didn't exist.

"I have to keep my eyes out for Ross and Neil." He pointed to the road, not letting on there could be even more dangerous men out there somewhere hunting her. She nodded.

"Like ye did last night with yer arm wrapped around some lass in a tavern."

Knowing he couldn't alienate her, because she was the only one who could answer his questions, he divulged part of the truth. "The lass was Ross's sister. I'd heard she was there, which was why I left ye at the inn and hurried over to catch her before she left. I wanted to learn if she knew why he and Neil attempted to kidnap ye."

Her pursed lips softened. "Did she ken anything?"

"Nae."

Looking away, she stared at something then turned back to him, fury blazing in her stare. "How well do ye ken her?"

"We are just friends."

"Like ye were just friends with Nora Stewart?"

Tilting his head, he gazed at her. *Where had that anger come from, and what the hell was she talking about?*

"I saw ye two together. It looked as if ye were asking her to marry ye." When he didn't say anything, she continued, "I was going to confront ye, but ye left the Cameron lands without a word and didnae come back. Were ye with Nora when my father was dying? Is that where ye were when ye would lie to me about where ye'd been?"

His fists clenched. *How could she think such a thing?* "Nae."

She was safer if she didn't know where he'd been disappearing to, but he couldn't let her go on thinking he'd been with Nora. He was going to have to get her to trust him before he could start questioning her on her uncle's allegiance and why Argyll might want her. Returning his stare to hers, he admitted, "Nora is married to my brother. There has never been anything between us. I dinnae ken what ye saw, but ye were wrong."

Her gaze softened. "Why should I believe ye?"

"Och, if ye cannae give me yer trust, ye can ask anyone back home."

"Then why would ye lie to me about where ye were?"

"There were things I had to do. I cannae even remember them now. 'Twas so long ago." That wasn't true; he remembered every one of his missions, but he couldn't trust her with the details. "But I promise, I wasnae with any other when I was with ye."

She nodded, seeming to believe him, then looked away and reached into the basket to pull out their much overdue meal.

A short time later, he tore off a bite of bread and popped it in his mouth. Smiling inside as she relaxed and took a piece of meat, he picked up their only flask of ale and offered it to her first.

She took a sip and handed it back. "Do ye remember the time we had too much of father's ale and got lost in the woods."

"Aye. 'Twas the day I discovered one of my favorite pastimes."

She grinned. "I just remember laughing and ye chasing me."

"Dinnae tell me ye forgot." She bit her lip and peeked at him through long, thick lashes as she struggled with the memory. Heaven help him, despite the way she'd treated him, he wanted to kiss her.

And what was wrong with that? They would have a few days together before they reached Kentillie. If intimacy helped her relax, and trust him enough to answer his questions about her uncle and Argyll honestly, why not? He'd learned how to separate himself and his emotions from the Raven's activities, so he'd have no trouble letting her go. The more she could tell him, the better the Raven could keep her safe, which was the most important thing he could do for her, and maybe she could provide the answers to help the Royalists and their clans.

Before he knew what he was doing, he'd inserted the cork back in the flask and tossed it to the side. His hand slipped to her side, and his fingers danced along her ribs on top of her gown.

Skye fell back onto the ground, laughing as she wriggled

to get free. He leaned in over her as the world around them disappeared.

He froze. Skye's bonny flushed cheeks and heated emerald eyes captivated and called to him. Her chest rose and fell as she struggled to rein in her breath. Her gaze darted to his lips, and she licked her own in an unspoken invitation, and he wasn't sure if he saw longing or fear in the depths of her eyes. If it was distress, she was paralyzed with it, because she made no move to free herself from her position pinned beneath him. Her touch on his arm became a faint whisper, a feather light caress that pulled at him, while at the same time, her eyes dilated. Her lips parted in an invitation he couldn't ignore.

His head dipped toward hers, and he could smell the smoky apple undertones of the ale they had shared, and knew it would taste even better on her lips.

She closed her eyes and tilted her chin to give him better access. As his mouth made contact with the soft velvet of hers, he gave in to the fierce need to claim what she was offering. His tongue darted into her mouth, and he scooped a hand under her back and drew her body to his. Pleasure spiked and raced through his limbs when her tongue reached out to dance with his.

Horses' hoofbeats and men's laughter reached him. Pulling back, he sat and whirled around to check the road. Hell.

A caravan with several men, a couple of women, and one small child rode by, innocent. But he couldn't lose control like that again.

Chapter Seven

Brodie kept watch on their surroundings but at the same time studied Skye. Spine stiff and shoulders straight, she broke a piece of bread and ate as delicately as if she were a lady in a castle.

Springtime of his seventeenth summer had been the last time the MacDonald had come to visit her while her father was still alive. Brodie had spent the whole day plowing the fields, making up the work his brothers had slacked on. Covered in filth and the mud left by days of relentless rain, he smelled of muck, sweat, and other things he didn't care to think about.

He and his brothers were almost home when Skye trotted up to him on the proudest mare he'd ever seen, all smiles in a new plaid of the deepest green, which matched her bonny eyes. Her shiny blond hair billowed around her shoulders as if she were a goddess straight out of the myths her father used to read to them.

The horse, which had been a gift from the MacDonald, had taken one sniff of him, snorted, and backed away, but

Skye didn't seem to notice the insult, or that of her uncle's as he nudged his horse toward hers as if to shield her from the common farmer blocking their path.

"Brodie, where were ye last night? I was expecting ye to come by," she asked.

"I kenned ye had guests and didnae want to intrude."

"Ye have to come with us to Kentillie. The laird has ordered a feast for Uncle."

"Nae," her uncle interjected as he nudged her to keep going. "Looks as if the lad has put in a full day and needs to clean himself and rest. The dinner is a small one, for family only."

Brodie didn't know what to say, just gritted his teeth. His uncle was the Cameron laird, and although he had that connection, he felt anything but regal in that moment.

Skye's lips pinched as if she would protest but then said, "I will see ye tomorrow, then."

He just nodded as they rode past, and his thoughts turned to how he would discover the truth about the man who looked down upon him and wished to give Skye to another.

Kerk, his oldest brother, sidled up next to him. "Did ye see that horse he gave her?"

"Aye," was all he could manage as he watched them ride toward the castle.

"'Tis plain he thinks ye arenae good enough for her." Brodie looked down at the calluses and new blisters forming on his hands. There was truth to the words. He turned to go, but his brother's next statement cut even deeper. "Ye ken ye will never be able to give her what she is accustomed to." His brother's voice held sympathy instead of the usual taunt, which made it even worse, so he kept going without looking back.

Kerk was correct. He would never be able to give her the luxuries her uncle could. She deserved someone better, but despite that knowledge, he couldn't let her go.

"I've heard the MacDonald laird is already planning a match for her," Kerk called to his back.

Vowing he would redeem himself, he'd decided then to take his uncle up on the offer to become a spy and work with Alex Gordon and the Royalist Resistance to prove to the MacDonald laird he was worthy. And if he found out that her uncle was a traitor to the Royalists, so be it.

That night, he became the Royalist Raven.

Skye didn't come to see him the next day or the several after that. Not until her uncle had gone did she find the time to seek him out, but by then, he'd been on his first mission. Because of its success, his resolve and his self-worth strengthened, minimizing the insecurities her uncle's visit had dredged up.

But his brother had been right, and all his efforts toward redemption didn't matter after Darach died. He'd been spying in Inverness when everything was taken from him.

The MacDonald had whisked her away, and when he'd tried to see her, he had near died from the beating. Then, he'd been given the news Skye was to wed a MacLeod. The union had never materialized, but it was enough for Brodie to realize Skye's infatuation with him had ended. Still, he'd always wondered what had broken her betrothal.

A soft hand touched his leg and brought him back to the present. Skye's. "Are ye all right?"

He nodded and shook off the memory.

They finished eating in silence, packed up, and were back on their way to Cameron lands shortly after. It would soon be time to find an inn and stop for the night. Still weary from lack of sleep and spending last eve in and out of the cold, he wanted to find them a place to stay before the nighttime chill settled in. He thought he heard rustling as they made their way through a narrow path between the trees, but an early evening mist had descended, and it was hard to distinguish anything in the trunks and brush.

An unfamiliar male voice ordered, "Halt right there."

Every muscle in his body tensed as his gaze darted around to take in the threat. Five men caked in filthy, frayed gray coats emerged from behind the trees at the side of the road. He felt Skye shudder.

Scanning the mounted men for weapons, he was happy to notice what they did have were rusted and far inferior to his own. The horses looked almost as pitiful as the men, with coats dull from illness, or lack of nourishment and care.

He wasn't sure whose land they were on, but he was fairly certain the men did not belong here. The ragged crew appeared as if they didn't belong anywhere, possibly exiled from some clan. "Are we on yer land? What clan are ye?"

All were thin but one, and each appeared haggard, as if they had been scavenging for a long time and had not been very successful at finding much during the harsher than normal winter.

"Campbell," the fat one with no hair shouted.

The leader cut his gaze toward the man with a threatening glance and put his finger up to his mouth as he shook his head.

The tip of a black flag with yellow writing hung from one horse—the standard of the Argyll's Regiment of Foot, the force responsible for the massacre on Rathlin Island. Men capable of unspeakable cruelties, who had pushed hundreds of Catholic MacDonald women, Skye's kin, over the cliffs to the rocks and surf below.

But this lot looked under-equipped, so perhaps they had been exiled from the Campbells. They must have done something fair awful if Argyll would let them go—the earl was desperate to hire whatever able-bodied men he could find so his Covenanters could wage war on the Royalist Resistance.

One man and a small lass probably looked like defenseless prey, but these scoundrels were going to be sorely disappointed. Aye, he appeared to be a rogue and simple farmer, but Brodie knew how to fight. Many nights he'd trained in secret, joining his cousin in the lists to learn the skills of all the Cameron guards.

Squaring his shoulders, he spoke with measured authority. "We are Camerons on our way home. We only seek to travel through."

The man in the middle, the obvious leader, stepped forward. He was larger than the rest, but still almost half Brodie's size. He wouldn't be a threat; it was just the number of them that concerned him.

The man's gaze traveled from him to Skye and raked across her as if the arse thought to claim her. When a shudder racked her, his blood started to heat, and he drew her closer.

"I'll be takin' the lass with me," the man lisped, and smiled to reveal a jagged row of stained, yellow teeth with a large gap, leaving the impression of a soulless ghost in the darkness.

Along with the grime on his face, he had a jaundiced appearance and large bulging eyes that reminded Brodie of a rat. Those reddened eyes skimmed up and down Skye as if she were a piece of meat and he hadn't eaten in weeks.

Brodie went into high alert. His fingers unconsciously dug into Skye's ribs as his arm tightened around her.

"She is my wife."

The arse laughed, a cavernous, guttural sound that raked Brodie's nerves. "She's worth a purse of gold. Leave her here and be on yer way, Cameron drunkard. I'll even give ye the money for a pint, and ye can find another wench."

Brodie muscles tightened as the men laughed. His breathing became heavy and measured when he realized there was more to the bandit's interest in Skye than to spar beneath the sheets with a comely lass. This blackguard would die before he touched her.

"We ken who she is." The man's eyes darkened as he turned a gaze filled with malice to Skye then spit in challenge. "Argyll wants her. 'Tis up to ye if we take 'er alive or dead."

Isobel had been correct.

"Nae, 'tis no' me." Skye was truly surprised.

The rat explained for him. "The order went out last night. Ye are Skye Cameron, niece to the MacDonald laird, no mistakin' that hair o' yers. 'And 'er over, wastrel, and we'll see you have coin for the closest tavern."

Now that Brodie realized she knew nothing of why Argyll wanted her, he wondered what Skye's uncle had done to cause the earl to set a bounty on her head. What would these bandits do if they knew he was number two on Argyll's infamous list of most wanted?

"Mayhap ye didnae 'ear me. We'll take the bitch, and ye can be on yer way."

Primitive fury exploded deep from his chest. It ignited a flame that could only be put out by destroying this threat to his woman. His only regret was that the man would not live long enough to grovel at Skye's feet with the apology she deserved.

"What does Argyll want with her?" If he found out why the arse wanted her, he might be better able to protect her. Staring the rat down, he kept the other men in his peripheral vision as they fanned out around them.

"He didnae say. Only said deliver the wench alive or dead."

"Ye willnae be taking her." Scenarios played out in his head of what they would do to Skye before delivering her into the devil's hands. He didn't even want to think on what the earl would do to her. What the hell had she become involved in?

Brodie could almost smell the man's fetid breath as he sneered through rotting teeth, "Draw yer sword, then. We cannae let ye pass."

The group had surrounded them, cutting off their path ahead and any chance of retreat. His only shot would be taking them on in hopes they would scatter and give Skye the opportunity to maneuver around the motley group. If he could do that, his horse would outrun them, and she would get to safety.

Without taking his eyes from the circling men, he whispered in Skye's ear, "If I fail, take off to Cameron lands and seek out Lachlan. This horse will get ye there. Dinnae stop anywhere."

Brodie dismounted then pulled the sheath from his back. In one solid movement, he drew the sharp glistening blade his father had given him on his eighteenth birthday from its case. It pierced the silence that had fallen and gleamed despite the dim.

He sorely wished he'd spent more time training in the lists; he was skilled with a blade, but out of practice since he had to train by night and feign ignorance by day. The squat, balding man on his left lunged first, wielding a sword that looked as if it had never seen the winning side of a battle.

It was the prideful man who wouldn't deny his clan. The man's strike was no match for him, and he deftly evaded the blow. The man was not patient, nor overly skilled as he returned to swing wildly, missing his mark every time. Argyll had been desperate, indeed, to enlist such men in his army.

"Take him, Hog," shouted one of the men standing by. Wheezing and snorting, the "Hog" was obviously out of practice as well.

Hog charged at him and raised his pitiful weapon, but instead of darting, Brodie stood his ground. He blocked the blow with a strong strike of his own. Under the force of his superior claymore, Hog's blade broke. The man's eyes widened and Hog hesitated. That split second allowed Brodie to swing again and strike just under the man's ribs. Hog froze, his snorting turning to a gurgling as he stared at the wound then collapsed to the ground.

Squaring his shoulders, Brodie stood his ground to face the next man foolish enough to make a move. He glanced over to see Skye still on the horse and covertly maneuvering around the melee to make her way up the road. *Smart lass.*

A red headed brute stepped up. "Yer goin' te die." This man was hardiest of the sickly bunch and looked to be the only one who would give him a fair fight. Brodie took up a defensive stance with knees slightly bent and sword held by both hands in front of his torso. The redhead's sword was polished and well cared for, and the man mirrored his stance, demonstrating skill and training.

"If ye go now, ye willnae meet his fate," Brodie said as he bounced slightly on his knees, preparing for the coming assault. Flexing his fingers, he shifted his superior sword back and forth from hand to hand.

"Hog saved me life." the man fumed through clenched teeth.

"Then dinnae let yerself be killed for his ignorance. I just want to take my wife and be gone," Brodie countered, knowing he was dealing with possibly the only sensible one of the group.

Hog gurgled again. Both their gazes shifted to the bandit writhing on the ground.

"No," screamed the redhead as Hog appeared to take his last breath.

Hog's friend turned cold eyes and rage on him. Strangely, he picked this time to notice the man's brows and hair were singed as if he'd been in a fire. The brute stomped forward to attack with a strong blow from the right. The strike was meant to hit just at Brodie's shoulder, but he was able to inch back in time to avoid the impact.

His angry opponent had not been able to control the swing of the blade, and when he stumbled on the follow through, Brodie swung over and came down with his blade on his opponent's back.

Doubling over and clenching his side, the man turned pale. Brodie recognized it as a killing blow and was surprised at how quickly he had taken the man down. He inhaled sharply to stay calm and keep a level head before facing the next challenger.

"Take him," the leader ordered, waving an overly ornate knife. Skye's gaze followed the amber encrusted hilt as if she were enthralled by it. It did seem a pricey piece for a bandit to possess, even if he had stolen it; he'd have thought they would have sold it for food. The scoundrel smiled triumphantly through his misshapen mouth as the other two men approached Brodie with swords drawn.

Molten fury coursed through his veins and quickened his pulse. He swung and cut the one on the right down in one blow, while the other man stared in horror at the blood spurting from his companion's shoulder and midsection.

Looking like he was just out of his youth, the smallest and least threatening bandit paled and turned wide eyes on him. The young one's arms shook as he attempted to hold up a sword that likely weighed more than he did.

A wail rent the air like the lingering sound of a horn. The leader screamed, "The bitch stabbed me."

Skye, who'd apparently slipped from the mount and bested the man, ran toward Brodie. The scoundrel attempted to catch her, but fell to his knees, dropping the knife and reaching for his side. Brodie's gaze returned toward the immediate threat.

The last man standing took one more look at his fallen

comrades and their writhing leader and bolted toward the rat, stopping only to scoop up his ornate knife and continue into the woods. Instead of chasing the thief, Brodie yanked Skye behind him so he was between her and the leader.

The man raised one red palm, and blood spurted from the wound as his disbelieving gaze drifted between Brodie and Skye. The dirk she'd used to slice meat at lunch was lodged in the rat's side.

Since the man on the ground did not appear to be a threat, Brodie turned to inspect Skye. Her limbs were limp. She stared at the man on the ground as he fell on his face.

She swayed, but he caught her before she collapsed. She looked at him with unfocused eyes, her breath uneven, then she pushed free and fell to her knees, gasping. He knelt beside her and rubbed her back, careful to keep one eye on the fallen man and the woods around them to make sure the last bandit didn't return.

Her body shook as he held her, but a rustling sound from the bandit leader pulled him back. What if the last one had run for reinforcements? They had to get out of there.

"Stay here, love." Reluctantly pulling her from his arms, he continued, "We must be on our way, but I need to clean up a bit." She nodded, but he did not think she really understood a word he was saying.

As the steeds were sickly and easily identifiable, he corralled the bandit's horses and encouraged them down the road back south. After dragging the limp bodies to the side of the road and retrieving and wiping clean the dirk Skye had used, he scooped her up and set her up on the horse.

"Are ye all right?" he asked. She nodded, but the vacant, far off look in her eyes told another story. He had to get her home and figure out how he was going to protect her from Argyll and his men.

He signaled for the horse to move, slowly at first so as not to jolt her, but then increasing speed. Away from the carnage, away from any danger. He didn't know how many more men were waiting in the woods. And there were still Ross and Neil to consider.

Despite the peril being with him presented, until Skye could be returned to her uncle's fortress, he was the only man that could keep her safe.

• • •

Trees whizzed past as their dark shadows grew longer and Skye shivered from the drop in temperature. This time of year, daylight was a commodity, and they had to take advantage of the warm rays before they faded into the evening.

Traveling at a fast speed was catching up with Skye, and her rear end hurt from the pounding of the horse, but Brodie was obviously trying to distance them from the violence.

He held her close, and she welcomed the embrace without question. He'd not judged her for putting a dirk in the man's side. The bandit was the man who had grabbed her in the tavern, and she realized they must have been following her. If not for her actions, Brodie might not be with her now. Sinking into him, she savored the feel of being held in his arms. His firm hold on her had remained steadfast, and he'd not uttered a word since they'd left the site of the brawl.

Fear for him had been her utmost concern. There had been two men attacking him as she dismounted and sneaked up on the leader. And Brodie had been magnificent. He did not even have a scratch, and she had been determined he would not be injured because he'd worried about her.

The sun's light dipped behind the trees. Hunger gnawed at her, and she had no idea where they were.

"Brodie," she said hoarsely.

There was no response as they cantered along. Clearing

her parched throat, she peeked back over her shoulder and tried again. "Brodie," she said, much clearer this time. "Why would the Earl of Argyll want me?"

Stirling was the first place she'd visited off MacDonald lands since leaving Cameron lands years earlier, and she couldn't think of anything she could have done to incur the earl's wrath. The Covenanter leader apparently wanted her dead, and she needed answers.

"I dinnae ken, but I think 'tis best if ye stay with me until we figure it out."

She nodded and accepted that she had felt safe back in the clearing with Brodie. He might disappear without explanations, but he had kept her well-guarded considering the odds against him.

"My uncle might ken what he wants."

"Are ye sure yer uncle isnae in league with him?"

"Nae. He would never side with Argyll."

Silence met her words, and she wished she could see what Brodie was thinking, but her position on the horse kept her from glancing into his eyes. He seemed to be holding something back.

"I'm starting to get hungry," she said after they'd ridden along for a while longer. Brodie slowed the horse to a trot, but he didn't say a word, so she continued, "'Twill be dark soon. How far do we have to go?"

"We will have to stop somewhere." His voice held a resignation that said if he had the choice, he would continue on through the night.

"Is there another inn?"

They had passed a few, but he had told her the less they stopped, the faster they would get back to Cameron land. She tilted back into him unconsciously.

A nostalgia for Kentillie castle had kept her thoughts humming this afternoon, as she reflected on the people she had left behind. Once they arrived, she would see her friend Donella again. They had corresponded over the last few years, and she knew the girl was now married with a bairn.

Would they still be as close? Before her uncle had dragged her to his home, Donella had been the only one she had been able to talk to about Brodie's absences. If she only had Donella with her on the Isle of Skye when the worst had come, then maybe she wouldn't be so afraid of being on her own. If she'd had someone to help her navigate through all the pain, maybe she would have been able to put it behind her. But she'd been alone, and the memory haunted her every day.

She let out a breath and pushed the long ago memory away. She didn't want to dwell on what she couldn't go back and change.

"Aye. 'Tis another inn no' too far ahead. We will stop for the night."

"I hope 'tis no' too late to get something to eat." Her stomach gurgled at the thought.

"I will make sure we find ye something."

"Brodie, thank ye for taking care of me back there." She had spent so much time being angry at him over the years, she'd thought the words would be hard, but once they spilled from her lips, a lightness engulfed her as some hidden pressure bubbled up to escape.

"I wasnae going to let anything happen to ye."

"I may have killed that man."

"Aye, love, but ye did the right thing. Sorry ye had to go through that."

Brodie's arm tightened around her waist, but she didn't want to think about how she had welcomed the embrace, or the kiss they'd shared earlier. How right it had felt to be in his arms with her lips pressed so intimately to his.

She had become lost, melting into him, her heart assuring

her that he was different and wouldn't leave her again. She felt protected, like he could and would defend her from this secret threat. He wasn't the insecure lad of his youth who'd allowed his family to push him around.

But he'd still not told her where he disappeared to frequently, and she was to wed another. Despite the desire to feel his touch again, she couldn't give in. She was to be married.

An inn slightly larger than the one they'd slept in last night appeared around a bend in the road. Billowing smoke puffed from one of the chimneys and welcomed them with the promise of shelter and food. Relief washed over her as Brodie slowed the mount.

A graying, plump woman greeted them after they had settled the horse and walked in the solid wooden door. "I'm Allina. Welcome to The Ruffled Feathers. Ye lookin' for some food or lodgin'?"

"Aye, we are in need of both," Brodie replied as Skye rushed over to the stone hearth where a fire blazed and crackled with dancing flames.

Brodie followed her with the lady in tow.

"Ye happen to be in luck. We have a room, and Patty just made up some venison stew."

"Do ye have a private dining area?" Brodie asked, standing nearby while he continued to speak with the woman, but the conversation faded as Skye scanned the room.

In one corner of the common area, a family with three small children supped. The mother was spooning small servings of the stew into one child's mouth. He rewarded her each time by clapping and opening his mouth again like a baby bird. The father was holding a small babe while the oldest, probably about five, banged the serving pieces on the table to try to divert the parents from their tasks. Skye tore her gaze away and skimmed the rest of the room.

A table was set up on an outer wall, and two well-kempt men, both with chestnut hair and the same nose, chugged ale as they waited for a meal. The inn's patrons seemed peaceful, reassuring company after dealing with the bandits.

"Skye." Brodie tilted his head for her to follow as the innkeeper's wife led them through a door just to the left of the large stone fireplace.

It opened into a small private dining area with its own hearth. She was delighted by the space, but disappointed that the peat was not lit. The room was cozy but cool.

"Give me just a moment, and I'll send in Ronan to get ye a blaze a'goin'."

"Thank ye," Brodie said as he took Skye's hand and guided her to a seat facing the fireplace. "We'll also take some ale and some of that stew."

"Aye, and I'll be right back with that ale," Allina said as she rushed from the room.

Skye had expected Brodie to take a seat across from her, but he sat in the empty chair beside her. The rhythm of her heart increased at his close proximity. His leg brushed against hers, and she became intensely aware of his nearness and the way it sent shivers through her.

Collin, Collin, Collin. She tried to think only of her betrothed, but with Brodie beside her, it felt even more intimate than riding curled up next to him on the horse all day. That was a forced closeness, but this was of his choosing. But then again, she didn't move to put distance between them. She must still be in shock from the idea that she'd killed a man.

After the day's events, she'd loosened her guard, but she had to remain wary. No matter how close they were becoming again, he was not for her. She tried to remember Collin's face, but all she could see was Brodie's.

He turned to her. "How are ye?"

I'm falling apart is what she thought, as she fought the need to lay her head on his shoulder and beg him to wrap his strong arms around her.

"Ye did what was necessary. I am thankful ye had the dirk with ye."

She blinked as his words sank in. Och, she was a fool. He was talking about the bandits, not her body's treacherous reaction to his nearness.

She shuddered. *Dirk, yes, that was mine.* But there was something about her attacker's weapon that looked familiar, like she'd seen it before. But that wasn't possible.

"Will ye be all right?" He studied her with a worried gaze.

"I will be once I have some food and rest."

Thankfully, Allina whirled back in with a tray, closely followed by a man with a cheery disposition to match hers. "I have some ale for ye and some cheese and bread while cook warms up the stew."

"I'm Ronan," said the man with her. "Pleased ye folks have stopped in for the night. I'll just get ye a nice fire goin' and let ye eat in peace." He winked at them.

Allina offered Skye a cup, and she took it. After a small tentative sip of the ale to test it, she was happy to discover it was smooth and warm. It soothed her parched throat and gave her hope that the food would be better than that of the last inn.

"'Tis verra good," she said, and Allina beamed.

Only moments later a blaze was roaring. She nibbled on cheese and enjoyed the ale until stew and more bread were brought in. It was perfect for the cool evening, comforting and familiar, reminding her of the many nights Brodie had eaten with her and her father when they were younger. As far back as she could remember, he had been part of her family, her hopes, and her future. Now those recollections were bittersweet. That time was so long ago, but the memories were still fresh enough to taunt her.

Brodie was uncharacteristically quiet, and she felt the need to fill the silence. "How is Donella?"

It had been the right thing to ask, because it brought him out of his silent brooding. He smiled. "She is well, and her babe has grown so much. He crawled fast and will probably be walking soon."

"I have to admit that I am looking forward to seeing them."

She projected the happiness, but her heart ached because she'd caught the gleam in his eyes when he'd mentioned the babe. Brodie had always loved children, and he'd told her how badly he wanted his own family and how he would be there for his sons, unlike his father, who was often away.

The memory angered her—he hadn't been there for her when she needed him. He was still evasive about where he had been. It was just a reminder that she couldn't trust this man.

"Ronald is a lucky man. They look so happy." His wistful gaze slid down and then back up to hers with an emotion she couldn't place. Was it real longing for her or a practiced seduction he used on every woman? Och, he knew how to knock a lass off balance.

Bounding back into the room, Allina held a small tray of tarts. Turning her attentions to the innkeeper's wife, Skye focused on a topic she always wanted to talk about— cooking. "The stew was perfect, Allina. The combination of mushrooms and sage was genius." Once Skye got back to the kitchens, she would have to try to replicate the recipe.

"Thank ye, lass. 'Tis one of Ronan's favorites. It has taken me years to get it right. Let me ken if I can get ye anything else. The second door on the left up the stairs is waiting for ye when ye wish to retire."

"Thank ye," Brodie said as Allina offered him a small curtsy and left.

"How is Lachlan? I heard he married." She picked up a piece of a tart and inhaled the buttery scent before taking a small bite.

Brodie's eyes lit and both dimples appeared. "Ah, he is smitten. After Eileen, I thought he would never find another, but Maggie suits him."

"He is a good man. 'Tis nice to ken he has found the right one."

"They are expecting their first babe."

"Do ye think they will be pleased to see me?"

"Aye, I ken they will." He reached out and took the hand she still kept on her lap. The touch was reassuring, and her head screamed at her to pull away, but her heart thudded and thrilled at the touch.

How did he still do that to her?

Reaching forward with the hand not clinging to hers, he tucked a stray tendril of her hair behind her ear. Heat crept up her cheeks, and her breath hitched, and she sat mesmerized as her defenses fell away.

Trailing his fingers down to under her chin, he tipped her head up, and she watched, helpless, unable to flee, as he moved in to place a sweet, gentle kiss on her lips.

Remembering her betrothed, she shook her head and leaned back to escape his touch as she took his hand from her face and placed it back on his own lap.

"I need sleep," she said as she stood and waited for him to do the same.

He rose, the look on his face anything but repentant. The corner of his mouth had curved up to reveal one of his dimples. Warmth spread through her, but she skirted around him and made her way to the stairs. The last thing she needed was for him to know how much he still set her heart racing.

Chapter Eight

Frantic knocks sounded in the hall outside their room, putting Brodie on alert as he halted pulling on his boots. He held his breath as he heard a door open and two men begin to speak in heated tones.

"Four dead," a weary, but angry voice stated.

A curse flew through the air, followed by something pounding on the plaster outside with such force that it vibrated through the walls of the old tavern. "Was it the MacDonalds again?" He'd heard this voice before but couldn't place it, and now they were talking about Skye's uncle's clan.

"Aye 'tis what it looks like. Angus wrote out MacDon in his own blood as he lay on the floor dying. 'Tis unspeakable to attack a family while they sleep."

"The brutal bastards. We have to put an end to it," said the familiar voice.

"I ken no MacLeans will sleep soundly until we do."

Brodie recognized the voice now—it was Ross MacLean's oldest brother, the man who would one day be laird.

Ice spread through him as he turned his gaze to Skye,

who had frozen, standing at the end of the bed in the process of dressing in a rosy pink gown he'd had delivered from the town seamstress the evening before. She eased down on the end of the bed, angling her ear toward the door.

The MacLeans were staunch Royalists. If Skye's uncle was attacking them, it could be the proof he needed that the MacDonald was a Covenanter sympathizer. The letter he'd given to the innkeeper on their arrival last night to be delivered to a post-boy invited the MacDonald laird to come retrieve Skye at Kentillie, but there was no way he'd let her go with a Covenanter, especially when Argyll wanted her dead.

A bang reverberated as a door shut, and Brodie assumed both the men went inside one of the rooms, because all he could hear after that were muffled tones. He could feign inebriation and listen as he lay outside the door. On numerous occasions, he'd had to put himself in a vulnerable position and suffered a few cracked ribs and bruises when he'd been kicked to make sure he was of no threat to the men talking. But Skye was here, and he couldn't put her at risk.

Could the men's discussion have something to do with Ross's attempt to abduct her? Instinct told him yes, and he didn't know if it was his duty or something more primal that warned him to keep her near. The MacLeans were a fearsome bunch when their clan was threatened, and someone out there was stirring them up.

And, what of the MacDonald? Was the man letting his clan run amok killing innocent people and threatening war? If he was in league with Argyll, why would the Covenanter leader be after Skye? The laird was more cunning than that and wouldn't risk his niece, but until Brodie knew the truth, he could trust no one. It would be all-out war between Ross's clan and the MacDonalds if Skye's uncle were truly involved in the massacre of innocent MacLean farmers.

In the meantime, Skye would most certainly be better off

with the Camerons at Kentillie—he'd have Lachlan lock her in the dungeon before he allowed her to put herself in that kind of danger.

The need to keep her guarded came back stronger than ever, but also the idea that she knew something which could help him put all the pieces together.

Standing without retrieving his boots, he moved to the end of the bed and pulled Skye to her feet.

"That was Ross's brother talking about yer uncle's clan."

The far off look that had settled into her eyes faded. "The MacDonalds would no' slaughter innocent people. I dinnae ken what they are talking about," she whispered, but he could hear the bite in her words at the accusation.

"It could explain what Ross wants with ye."

"And what would that be?" Putting her hands on her hips, she glared at him with the same anger that had emanated from her the night he'd found her in the wagon.

"Mayhap revenge or as a bargaining chip to keep yer uncle in line." The trust he'd slowly developed with her over the last couple days was slipping away, but he continued.

"My uncle has done nothing." She started to put space between them, but he moved to the side and blocked her escape.

"Then, why does Argyll want ye dead? Mayhap the MacDonald made a deal with him to slaughter innocent Royalists but his conscience returned, so he's stopped following the earl's orders."

"My uncle would never bow down to the Covenanters." They glared at each other for a moment. He backed away but kept his gaze on her as she darted to the other side of the room.

He would have to resort to an indirect method to gain information. As he'd surmised earlier, seduction was his best course of action. It would be easier than this verbal sparring.

Motioning for Skye to continue dressing, he peered out

the small window and saw that the MacLeans were mounting their horses and riding away. It was safe to leave the room. But as they made their way downstairs, he eyed every corner and crevice they passed for any potential threats.

• • •

As they sped along the well-trodden road back toward Skye's old home and the world she'd left behind, the time passed quickly and dark pines became thicker, dotting the inclines of the mountains as they started to take on familiar forms. The terrain had become a bit rougher and the trail made snake-like patterns, slithering around the landscape to adjust for the steep hills and fast flowing streams.

The conversation of the men in the hall this morning played again in her head, and she couldn't help but think she was missing something important. Brodie must have felt the same, because he'd turned confrontational, accusing her uncle of awful deeds he was incapable of, which had only fired her temper. Brodie had no right to be angry with her.

What had they said? *"MacDon..."* Her head swirled as warning bells she couldn't quite hear rang out.

The murder of a MacLean had her thoughts wandering to Murdina, the woman who had taught her which spices mixed well and how to use them.

Who had told Murdina what happened to her husband? Skye could still see his brutalized body lying on the shore after she and her uncle had ferried across the waters that separated the Isle of Skye from the rest of the Highlands on their way to Stirling. Vicious cuts had marred his naked body, almost as if he'd been tortured. Blood still seeped into the ground where he lay face down, holding a stick with which he had etched some letters into the sand. She saw them, but they didn't register then, because she'd noticed his face and realized she knew him.

Memories of the man bringing in sacks of potatoes and other heavier items into the kitchen flowed through her, and she'd turned her head to block the sight, but the image was already burned into the back of her eyelids. She thought of the three fatherless children and the sweet woman who had been a mentor.

Her uncle had sent her ahead with a few men to an inn, where they'd stayed waiting for several days. When he arrived, he didn't answer any of the questions she'd put to him.

A shiver ran through her, and she had a nagging sense she should have caught on to something.

As the sun started to descend yet again, a loud yipping call erupted into the air, alerting them to the presence of a nearby fox in search of a mate. The sound took her back to the first time Brodie had gone somewhere and left her behind.

"Brodie, I have something to show ye," a younger version of herself called out to him as he boarded a wagon with his family. Having found a den of baby foxes, she wanted to share the discovery with him.

"No' now. I'll see when we get back." She wanted to scream "look at me," but his family was there, and his mother had never given the impression that she liked Skye. Not wanting to incur Shona's wrath, she tamped down the rising swell of anger.

"Back from where?"

"We're going to Inverness." She opened her mouth to ask why, but Brodie's father called out to the horses and they shot off, leaving her in clouds of dust.

The next morning, she'd gone to see the wee animals, but all she found were smudges of blood and a nest that looked as if it had been ripped apart. She cried alone in the woods, and when Brodie returned home, more than a week later, he didn't even ask what she had wanted to show him.

Looking back now, 'twas probably silly to have expected him to remember her request, but at the time, it had been important to her. Shaking her head free from the memory, she reflected on his uncharacteristic silence thus far on today's journey. She knew she'd upset him with her words this morning, but he was wrong about her uncle.

They had used most of the daylight to traverse the rocky winding path, but the sun's rays were fading behind the mountains now, and a cold breeze swirled, so they stopped at yet another inn for the evening, and she sought out the innkeeper while Brodie saw to the horse in the stables. Luckily, she'd been able to secure a room for each of them above stairs. She kept her distance and her resolve to not give in to the desire for the companionship, trust, and love they once shared. She was betrothed. Even if she found a way to forgive Brodie, it was too late for them. With Collin, she wouldn't have love, but she'd never be alone again, and Brodie had proven he couldn't give her that.

Setting out the next morning, she noticed Brodie's cheeks were flushed red, and he moved slower than he had the day before. By the afternoon, a bitter wind blew down the path, corralled by the mountains on either side. Dark gray clouds colored the sky in an ominous portent of what it intended to unleash on them.

Brodie pulled an extra plaid from a bag he'd had belted to the horse and wrapped it around them.

"We arnae far now. I dinnae have much in the kitchens, but I would be grateful if ye would make us something to eat." They hadn't stopped for lunch, and she was famished.

"I'm sure I can find something, but will yer mother let me in her kitchen?"

"Ye dinnae have to worry with that. I moved out."

Relief flooded her, and her rebellious mouth opened to confess something that had bothered her for years. "I dinnae think yer mother liked me."

"Nae, she liked ye just fine until ye left me without a word. Now, she isnae too pleased with ye. What makes ye think she didnae like ye?"

"She told me once that I was in the way and should spend more time at home."

"I promise that until ye left, she never uttered a word against ye."

They fell into silence again as thick white flakes filled the air, landing on her cheeks and hair, welcoming her home with the beautiful, magical twilight. An urge to go down the dark, moss covered path that led to the double waterfall she'd loved as a child brought a smile to her lips, but it was freezing. Those falls had brought her comfort whenever Brodie disappeared, the soothing hum blocking out the fear he wouldn't come back this time. She shook away the memory.

Shivering, she sank deeper into Brodie—he was like an oven and had kept her warm most of the day. But the cold had intensified with the wet slivers as the sun had started to set. A layer of white blanketed everything in sight, giving the landscape a dreamy, surreal view.

The snowcapped mountains and pines were beautiful, and despite her being gone for so long, it was reassuring to note the familiar landmarks dotting the frozen wilderness. She had never admitted to herself how much she truly missed this place, but seeing it again told her it had been a mistake to not insist her uncle bring her for a visit so she could deal with the demons of the past.

They rode past Brodie's house and kept moving toward the cottage where she had grown up, and her heart started to race with excitement. He was taking her home. Her toes were starting to go numb from the cold, and she leaned back closer to his warm body as he softly wrapped his arm around her waist.

"Welcome home."

She had expected to see a rundown shell of the home she had known from her youth, but it appeared just as well kept as ever, with its solid thatch roof and smooth stone walls still looking the same as the day she had left. Someone had cared for the place. Emotions washed over her as pride swelled in her chest and nostalgic memories danced through her head.

Her eyes watered, and she stood unmoving in the cold to enjoy the view while Brodie stabled the horse. An image flitted by, a young girl with bouncy blond curls skipping behind a golden haired braw Highlander—her father—and the tears threatened to spill.

Brodie joined her, but his movements had become slower and even more languid. Lines creased his brow, and his eyes were red and tired. She'd had chances to doze on their travels, but he had not, and now she felt guilty that he had pushed so hard to get them there in record speed.

Cold seeped through her boots as they trudged through the accumulating snow. When the door swung open, she gasped. It was as if she'd never left. One of her favorite plaids was draped across the back of the same wooden bench where her mother had read tales of chivalrous knights and ladies to her.

Skye darted into the house then walked in a daze to the red and green woven material. Sinking onto the worn cushions of the bench, she pulled the plaid up to her cheek. It was as soft as she remembered it, but the smell was different. The masculine scent of fresh chopped wood mixed with smoke filled her nostrils. *Brodie.* Her insides warmed. Not a thing had been changed, and it had all been meticulously kept up.

As the door clicked closed, she turned to him. He smiled, but it did not reach his eyes. He studied her.

"Did ye take care of it?" She waved her hand around the room.

"Aye," he said as he dropped the small bag he'd been carrying, then swiveled to latch the door. When he twisted back around he stumbled, and she'd have thought him intoxicated if she'd not just spent the whole day on horseback with him.

"Ye kept it all the same?" Her eyes followed him as he staggered to the cushioned bench beside her and fell into the seat.

"Aye, 'twas perfect the way it was. It has only been missing ye." His glassy eyes were sad and seemed to have trouble keeping their focus.

"Thank ye." Reaching out, she placed her hand on his cheek, wanting him to know how much it truly meant to her.

He was so hot.

"Ye're so warm. Are ye well?"

"I am just a wee bit tired. Let me get the fire going for ye."

"Nae, stay here." She motioned around the cottage. "I remember where everything is." Her uncle had not bothered to give her time to pack, because he'd whisked her away immediately following her father's funeral, insisting he would get her everything she needed.

Brodie remained seated without protest and curled up in the plaid she'd just been holding. Reclining awkwardly, his feet hung off the end as he lay on his back. The fabric rippled as he settled beneath it. He must not be feeling well to let her take charge.

Unease about his condition pricked at her, but she busied herself making a fire. She put some water on to heat for tea and was struck by a feeling of belonging. It felt good to be in her own home again. She inhaled sharply and reveled in the familiar smell of pine and peat.

Glancing over to where Brodie was softly snoring on the bench she smiled and was surprised by the first thing that popped into her head. He looked right there, too. This place was not her home without him in it. They had practically grown up together, and her father had loved him as much as he had her.

She tiptoed over to study him. The man who had once owned her body and soul. Being honest with herself, she sighed and admitted what she had tried to deny—he still did.

His teeth were chattering, and he was shivering. His golden skin had become pale. She knelt beside his restless form and touched his cheek again. Trailing her hand up, she gasped at the heat that radiated from his temple.

He was ill. Panic enveloped her. How had he become so sick so quickly?

Oh God. Her heart sank. He hadn't. The signs had been there all day. But he'd fought through it to get her home by tonight. The foolish man. She knew how to use herbs for cooking, but not how to heal.

Her hands trembled as she stood and clasped them together to calm the fear and helplessness that coursed through her. She had to find someone who would know what to do.

Would Coira still be at Kentillie Castle? The sun had almost set, but she knew the way by heart.

She raced to the kitchen and took the warming water out of the hearth. After gathering a plaid, she threw it on then struggled to pull her still wet boots back onto her feet. She knelt and whispered in Brodie's ear, "I'll get ye help, dearest."

It was the first time she had used that word in years. The old endearment had rolled off her tongue without thought. She swiped the tear back from her cheek, pulled at her arisaid, pinning it securely, and made her way to the door.

Once back out in the chilled night air, she ran for the stable. She would be able to get to the castle, but once she arrived, would there be anyone who would be able to help Brodie?

Chapter Nine

"Is Coira here?" Skye huffed and held her side as she ran into a room littered with several tables and chairs, along with a neat row of empty beds. A strong, medicinal smell lingered in the air.

Memories of the last time she'd been here intruded. Brodie had carried her through the door—she had been the one injured that day. Her foot. He had been chasing her after she'd promised him a kiss if he caught her. She was fast, but no match for his long legs and she had known it when she'd teased him, secretly hoping he would claim her lips.

Just as he was reaching for her, she'd stumbled. Her foot had turned as it stuck in a divot in the field at an odd angle. Blocking out the pain, she said nothing, because she had wanted that kiss. It had not disappointed. Her toes still curled at the memory of his hard body pressing her into the soft lavender. His brown eyes sparkling with mirth as her body heated to his touch had been worth not giving in to the discomfort.

When she rose to stand, though, her foot caved beneath

her weight, and she couldn't deny the injury. Brodie sat with her while Coira poked and prodded, then he'd held her hand as she'd pulled her slipper off and wrapped her ankle with cloth. He'd looked as if he'd pass out. At the time, she thought it odd that such a large, powerful man would be so squeamish, but now she knew better. It had been guilt and worry roiling in his gut, just as it did in hers now.

"Coira isnae here. I am Maggie. Can I help ye?" A bonny, black-haired lass she'd never seen before stuck her head out from the adjoining room to greet her. Skye ran forward, grasped the lass's hand, and stared into the beauty's startling sapphire gaze.

"I am—"

"Skye!" a woman exclaimed. A face she knew—Lorna—grabbed her in a tight embrace. "When did ye get here? Donella will be so happy to see ye." She pulled free to look in her old friend's eyes.

"Just now. I need help," she pleaded. "'Tis Brodie. Something is wrong." Her hands clasped over her mouth. She was not as brave as he had been that long ago day when he'd carried her in.

"What's wrong with Brodie, Skye?" Maggie gently placed a hand on her shoulder.

"He is so hot. He was shivering in his sleep. And he's pale. Can ye help? Please. I dinnae ken what to do." Her chest ached and felt as if it would cave in on itself.

"Let me get my bag. I'll go," Maggie reassured her. She turned and started grabbing items from a nearby table and throwing them into a well-worn sack.

"Lachlan willnae want ye to go out in this weather," Lorna clucked, shaking her head. Ah, this Maggie was the one Brodie told her about, the one whom the Cameron had married.

"Then will ye fetch him? He can go with me," Maggie

said in a calm but defiant tone, rolling her eyes where only Skye could see it.

"Aye. Good idea." Lorna breathed and bolted from the room.

Skye wrung her hands together and paced back and forth.

As Maggie collected more items, she peppered her with questions. "How long has he been feverish?"

Skye froze, and her eyes widened as she shook her head. How had she been so oblivious to his condition?

Maggie repeated the question. "How long has Brodie had the fever?"

"I dinnae ken." She admitted. "We were traveling all day. He did seem sluggish this morning, but I thought he was just tired. He had been quiet yesterday, too. That isnnae like him."

Maggie smiled. "Ye are quite right. He does tend to go on. Especially when he is talking about ye."

Skye froze. "He has spoken of me?" Her words were barely audible.

"He mostly goes on about what ye were like growing up. I can tell he still loves ye."

"How is that?"

"His eyes light up when ye are mentioned. 'Tis the only time I see true emotion on him." She couldn't think of a response. "Och, the tales Lachlan has told me about when ye left. Brodie fair near went mad, from what I hear. That is until…" Maggie pinched her lips together.

Skye's heart skipped a beat. Had he truly hurt as much as she had? And, until what?

Lachlan rushed in. "Skye." He embraced her quickly and pulled back. "Where is he, and where did ye come from?"

• • •

Skye's heart seized when they entered the house. He wasn't where she'd left him. Running to her father's room, she called out, "Brodie," then checked the room that had been built on as a spare. Not there, either. She rushed into her own room and found him on the bed, still wrapped in the green and red plaid, curled up in a ball.

"In here," she yelled to Maggie and Lachlan.

She took a step toward the bed and froze. Peeking out from beneath the well-worn material, he clutched something familiar. Gooseflesh rose on her arms as she looked closer and recognized a corner of the fabric object. It was a pillow she'd once made. Disliking needlework, she had been forced to sit with visiting family and learn on that cushion. Before her cousins and grandmother had gone back to Skye, she'd already planned the demise of the offending object, which she'd told Brodie as they skipped rocks by the loch.

He had talked her into giving it to him so her father wouldn't catch her in the act, and one day, she'd slipped it to him as he'd left their cottage. He had kept it, and now had it here in her bed.

"Skye," Maggie startled her. "'Twas yer home and ye ken yer way around it?" She nodded. "Good, we will need some water heated. Can ye start with that, then bring some clean rags and another light blanket."

She dashed from the room, thankful to be doing something to help.

When she returned with the items, her hands were no longer shaking. Maggie guided her through what she would need to do during the night to try to keep his fever down. The woman was skilled, and her confidence instilled in Skye a belief that Brodie would regain his health.

"Come, let him rest," Maggie said and gestured toward the door for her to follow.

She refrained from pointing out that he had not awakened

with all their attentions, and that she didn't want to be away from his side for a moment. Heart pounding at the thought of leaving him unattended, she followed Maggie out, silently vowing to Brodie to return soon.

Lachlan, who had waited in the main room, took his wife's hand and kissed it as his gaze traveled up and down to inspect the lass. Maggie looked tired, but she pulled her shoulders back and smiled, likely in an attempt to not show fatigue to her husband. He did not appear fooled.

Cutting concerned eyes to Skye, he said, "I will send food in the morning. I looked through the cabinets and there isnae much here."

"Thank ye." When she glanced back to Maggie, Skye's voice shook as she asked, "What should he eat?"

"Mostly liquids. Soup is good. But ye will also need something to keep up yer strength. Ye look so thin. Do ye ever eat?" She tilted her head and her lips pursed almost imperceptibly.

"I do when I cook."

"Ye like to cook, then?"

"I do." She straightened and smiled for the first time in hours.

"We will send enough to stock the kitchen, then. No telling how long this storm will last. I am getting hungry myself, so I'll stop by the kitchens on the way in."

Lachlan laughed, "Ye seem to always be hungry."

"'Tis cause I'm expecting his bairn." With pride, Maggie caressed her swollen belly, as Lachlan's arm pulled his wife in close. A pang of longing hit Skye before she allowed herself to be happy for the couple. They looked so perfect together, and she couldn't begrudge them their good fortune.

Fighting back the irrational jealousy that tried to claw its way in, and the familiar lump that caught in her throat when she saw another woman with a babe, she smiled. Lachlan deserved happiness after what he had been through, and Maggie seemed like a genuinely nice person. She'd come all the way out here on this dreadful night to help Brodie. Most people so large with child would not have ventured this far in the snow. Sparing a glance at the window, she noticed that large white flakes continued to come down at a steady pace.

"Thank ye for helping me with Brodie. I have never seen him like this before."

Panic swelled, and she thought for a moment to beg them to stay, to let them know how scared she was, and that last time she'd been left in this house alone, her father had died and she'd had no one.

"He will be fine. Just give him a little time." Maggie broke free of Lachlan's hold and wrapped Skye in a warm, reassuring embrace.

"We'll send some supplies as soon as we can," Lachlan said as he pulled his wife toward the door.

"Thank ye."

Deciding it was selfish to ask them to stay, she held her tongue, although she considered telling them to send her cousin Alan. But none of them would be safe out in that weather.

After they walked out, Skye bolted the door and rushed back to the room to check on Brodie. He hadn't moved, so she tiptoed to the kitchen to prepare the tea and compresses to pull down his fever.

Spending the next several hours wiping his forehead with cool rags and fretting over every little sound he made, she berated herself again for not noticing his condition earlier and for not insisting he rest instead of rushing them through the cold to get back. A couple of times during the night, she attempted to rouse him enough to get him to drink the special concoction Maggie had left, but it was no use.

When she wasn't trying to tame his temperature, she

explored her old home. Little things had changed, but most had stayed the same. Standing in the doorway, but not going in, she stared at her father's room, which still held the same blankets, cherry furniture, and his belongings, neatly placed in the same spots where he had kept them.

Her room was the biggest difference. Brodie had brought his own items in, and they were mixed in along with hers. He hadn't taken her father's larger room or cleared out hers, but moved into the smaller space. That thought melted some of the ice that had accumulated in her heart.

A few times, Brodie thrashed around in the grip of the fever and talked of Royalists and ominous plots, then he'd say her name.

Why had she not forced her uncle to bring her back to confront Brodie? Could she have been wrong about him? And how could she have promised herself to another when her heart was still here?

In the wee hours of the night, his fever subsided, and she was finally able to relax. There was nothing left to do but wait, so she lay down beside him and started talking, even though she knew he wouldn't hear. "I cannae believe how much I have missed this place. There are so many memories here, and most of them include ye."

She ran her fingers through his hair, enjoying the texture of his thick chestnut locks. Her heart skipped a beat when she remembered the last time they had been in her bed together. If only fate had not sought to keep them apart. She shut her eyes and tried to remember her obligations.

Och, her poor uncle was probably worried sick. He might very well murder someone over her disappearance.

• • •

Tap, tap, tap tap.

Brodie's eyes opened to a familiar ceiling, but something was different from every other morning he'd woken in this place. Skye lay beside him on the bed.

How had he come to be here? Was it a dream? If it was, he didn't want to wake.

He reached out and touched her arm—she was real.

Tap, tap tap.

Sparing a glance at the window, he saw there was light outside, but it was muted by a continuous fall of thick white snow.

A heavier *tap, tap, tap* sounded, and he would yell for whoever it was to go away, but he didn't want to startle the warm, sleeping lass who nestled up next to him like he was still her world. Reluctantly sliding out of the bed, careful not to wake her, he pulled the blankets up to her shoulders.

Cursing, he stumbled toward the noise, surprised at how a haze cluttered his vision and left his limbs feeling heavy and sore. His head pounded as if he'd been drinking all night, and his muscles ached as if he had been run over by a wagon.

"Who's there?" he called out when he got to the door, surprised by the hoarseness in his throat.

"'Tis yer cousin."

Lachlan.

Unlatching the door to admit his cousin, he was surprised by the knee-deep snow outside. He vaguely remembered getting home with Skye last night as the white flakes pelted them, but everything after that was foggy and unclear.

"Are ye feeling better, then?" Lachlan questioned as he kicked his boots on the doorframe.

Alan bustled in behind Lachlan with a large basket and set it on the table.

"What are ye doing?" Brodie scratched his head. Maybe he *was* dreaming.

"We brought ye and Skye some supplies. Ye will need it

with this weather," Lachlan answered.

"Where is Skye? I havenae seen her yet." Alan's gaze shifted around the room.

"How did ye ken we were here?" Brodie squinted and scooted over to a chair and sat. The room had started to spin, and his head felt heavy. He wanted them to leave so he could lie back down, but they seemed to know something.

"Skye came to Kentillie and found Maggie last night. I dinnae recall ever seeing her so worked up over something." Lachlan's brow's rose as if to hint there was some hidden meaning behind his words.

"I dinnae remember any of this." Brodie rubbed his hand over his dry eyes. Leaning back in the familiar chair, he blinked hard then opened his lids wide.

"Aye, when we got back here with Skye, ye were out. Feverish and delusional. Ye are looking a wee bit better this morning."

"Well, where is she?" Alan frowned. "Last time I went to the MacDonald's, I barely saw her."

Brodie looked at him and glowered as Alan's duplicity came to light. He came full awake and snapped out the words as his fists clenched around the arms of the chair. "Ye saw her and didnae tell me?"

"She is my cousin, Brodie. She asked me no' to tell you." Alan shrugged.

"Ye are my friend. Does that no' count?" Brodie was on his feet, shoulders thrown back. He took a step toward Alan, and the room started to swirl.

Alan held up his hands. "She just looked so sad when yer name was brought up." His gaze shifted down. "'Twas like all the life drained out of her. I didnae want to cause her any more pain."

"And ye thought I would do that?" Brodie shook as his jaw tightened.

"I just ken talking about ye made her unhappy. She would always ask if ye were still hopping from one wench's bed to the next. I couldnae tell her the truth without revealing your secret, so I just stopped talking to her about ye."

"Ye should have told me."

"Told ye what? That she was miserable. What would ye have done? No lass wants to ken the love of her life cannae control his baser needs, but if she knew the truth, she'd be in danger. Once ye turned spy, ye kenned she would no' be safe with ye."

Alan, his laird, and Lachlan's brother Malcolm were the only Camerons who knew of his double life, and it was best kept that way. Even so, when Skye had left him, there was a short time when he'd lost control and indulged in anything, be it alcohol or lasses, to make the pain go away for just a little while. That's why his persona was brilliant—it truly had been who he had become when Skye left.

"Aye, I was spying before, but I would have stopped. I wouldnae have remained the Raven had she stayed," he thundered, losing his temper. "Skye's the only one I ever wanted. The other wenches were all after she left."

"Have ye ever considered mayhap that is how she thought ye saw her, as just one of those wenches?"

Brodie's heart plummeted to his gut at something he'd never once contemplated. Was that what she thought?

Alan continued, "Yer reputation with the lasses is legend in the Highlands. Did ye think she wouldnae hear of yer exploits?"

"She left me before any of that."

Could she really have known so much about his spiral downward and then the duplicity of his life?

"Enough." Lachlan scowled at both of them. "We need to get back. Ye should have all ye need to get ye through the next few days. The snow is still falling, and I want to get back before we get stuck out here."

Brodie opened his mouth to give Lachlan a report on why they were here—Argyll's bounty on Skye, his plan to wed a Campbell lass to a MacPherson, that they needed to get word to The MacDonald, and the plot to destroy the Royalist lairds at an upcoming meeting in Edinburgh—but he was interrupted.

"Skye." Alan's face lit up.

Brodie turned to see a vision that made his heart leap. Standing in the doorway, still sleepy eyed, was Skye, wrapped in the plaid he'd draped over his body on countless occasions, with her silky blond hair tumbling down her shoulders. Bare feet peeked from beneath the worn edges of the green wool, a pattern that set off her emerald eyes and beckoned him to take her in his arms and carry her back to bed.

He'd been hoping to get back to that warm haven before she woke, wanted to enjoy the sight and feel of her waking up in his arms. He hoped she had not overheard their heated exchange, but it was probably what had roused her.

Alan rushed by him, scooped Skye up in his arms, and twirled her around. "It's been too long."

"Aye, it has," she returned with a smile as Alan set her back on her feet and steadied her with his large hands around her small middle.

Fury ignited. He would blame it on jealousy, were Alan not her cousin. But it went deeper than that. At one time, Brodie had lived for that smile—the one she no longer bestowed on him, but came so easily for others.

"'Tis time ye came for a visit. What finally got ye back home?"

She shot Brodie a look and raised an eyebrow.

"'Twas no' planned. But I am happy to be here." She turned to Lachlan. "I forgot to ask last night. How is yer mother? I cannae wait to see her."

Brodie grinned at her deft maneuvering of the conversation.

"She will be so pleased to see ye," Lachlan answered.

Alan finally let go of her waist and backed up slightly. They had always been close cousins, and that had not bothered him when they were younger. But now, he reflected on the times he'd asked after her and how each time, Alan had dodged the subject.

"If ye want, I will take ye to Kentillie to see her now." Alan tilted his head down to Skye's then slid a plotting gaze toward him with a slight slant of the head.

Now, he wanted to punch her cousin. If Alan messed up Brodie's chance to get to the truth about the MacDonald, and his few moments left with Skye, he would kill the man—her cousin or not. Swaying, he extended his arms to catch his balance.

"I will see her when it clears up outside. I think Brodie needs someone here. He still looks quite pale, and I havenae had the chance to make him the medicine Maggie instructed me to give him."

"Ye are certain?" Alan didn't let up.

"Aye," she said.

Alan embraced her again and turned toward Brodie, pinning him with an unveiled threat. His supposed friend mumbled so only he could hear as the Highlander walked by him, "If ye hurt her again, ye will have me to deal with."

His nails dug into his palms. It was all he could do not to strike out at Alan. He would never do anything to hurt Skye.

"When the weather is cleared, I am sure Maggie will want to have ye at Kentillie to welcome ye back," Lachlan interjected and, sensing the tension, placed himself between Alan and Brodie. Lachlan opened the door, and a chill breeze blew in, along with several hundred large snowflakes. "Let's get back, Alan."

"Thank Maggie for the supplies," he called after them, and then the door shut, leaving him alone to try to close the chasm between him and Skye.

He knew he had other information he'd wanted to give Lachlan, but his thoughts had hazed over and his body began to ache.

Chapter Ten

"Ye still look feverish. How are ye feeling?" Skye walked to Brodie and placed her hand on his temple.

Her hands were cold, but despite that, she could tell he still had a fever. His head felt as if he'd been bathing in the warm rays of the sun on a summer day.

"I amnnae certain. I dinnae remember what happened last night. I am happy to see ye still here and that ye didnae leave."

Did he think she would have left him in the shape he had been in? Wincing, she recalled his heated tone when she'd crept down the hall toward the men's voices. *"Skye's the only one I ever wanted."* She had heard the anger etched in those words. She had been so distraught when her uncle had taken her away that she had never given him the chance to explain.

He wavered and she pushed away the guilt to study later as she moved in to hold him steady.

"Sit," she ordered as she helped him to a cushioned chair. "I'll make a fire and get ye some of the medicine Maggie left. Ye still look pale, but I'll take that over yer condition last night." She went to the table and picked up the container Maggie had left, measured the correct amount into a smaller vial, then walked back over to Brodie. She held it out. "Drink." Thankfully, he downed the liquid without protest.

His lips puckered as he handed back the container.

"Och, what did she put in that?" Despite the sour face, his boyish charm made it amusing. She giggled. It was the first time she had done so and really enjoyed it in recent memory. "Ye rest. I'll put things away and make us something to eat."

"I can help." He started to rise, but she shook her head.

"Nae, ye need to get better. Looks like we are stuck with each other for a couple of days." The wolfish grin that greeted her reply made her blush as her insides warmed. "Dinnae get any ideas. I am here to see ye get well. Then, ye will have to take me back to my uncle."

As she put the items in the baskets away, she was struck again by how little inside the house had changed. Why had Brodie kept it all the same? Was it because he was never here, or had he purposely made as few changes as possible? He'd also been sleeping in her bed. Why not her father's much larger room, which would have suited him better?

Returning to the room with a steaming bowl only moments later, she noticed him leaning back with his eyes shut, but he didn't look peaceful. His cheeks were red, and he looked drawn. She placed the oatmeal pudding with cream, honey, and a berry compote on the small table where they had eaten so many times before, and tiptoed over to him.

Brodie's chocolate-brown eyes opened when she neared. When his face lit with a sleepy, innocent smile, she had the urge to lean down and kiss him, but instead, she put the back of her hand to his cheek. He had warmed once again. "Ye must get up and eat. Then I'll let ye rest."

Taking his hand, she pulled him to his feet to draw him to the table. Once he was seated, she went back to the kitchen for her own bowl then plopped down in a chair across from him.

"This is delicious," he said after he'd swallowed.

She blushed. "Thank ye."

"Where did ye learn how to cook like this?"

"In the Cairntay kitchens. I didnae ken anyone when I first got there, so I threw myself into cooking because I loved all the people being about. It has become a passion over the last few years."

"I can tell. 'Tis the best oatmeal pudding I have ever had."

She tried to contain the pleased smile by blowing on a portion and spooning a bite between her lips.

"Did ye find a man on Skye?"

She froze, finding it hard to swallow, and when she did, the oatmeal stuck in her throat. How could she tell him she was to wed another, when what she really wanted was to stay right here with him, despite all the past hurts and the possibility that she would end up alone. She opted for half the truth.

"Nae. I didnae find another at my uncle's home. Cooking became my passion. I wasnae looking for a man."

She should try to make him jealous after the years of hearing about his lecherous ways, but she couldn't bring herself to tell him she would soon be a MacPherson. For some odd reason, it was important he know she had thus far remained faithful to her childhood love.

"Will ye never marry, then?"

She gulped. "Uncle has determined 'tis time I take a husband. That is why he took me to the wedding at Stirling."

"Did ye find a husband?" His spoon stilled midair, and she thought he stopped breathing.

"There is a man my uncle has in mind." His slackened jaw had her confessing more than she should have. "'Tis for the good of the MacDonald clan."

When he didn't reply, she filled the silence. "What were ye doing in Stirling?"

"I went to the wedding with my family. They will be pleased to see ye when they return."

"And I them, but I fear this weather will delay everyone. The snow still falls at a steady pace."

She was surprised at how they fell into a comfortable discussion just like old times; he was still easy to talk to, despite the years they'd been separated. It was comfortable, and he seemed to be feeling better, so they moved to the cushioned bench where the conversation kept going for hours.

Later, she made lunch, a vegetable soup with potatoes, leeks, and carrots. Maggie had sent her an array of spices, and she was able to toss in a few to liven it up.

"Ye look tired," she observed as they moved back to the table, and she handed him the bowl.

"I do feel verra tired." He dipped a spoon into the soup and brought it up to his lips. He blew and steam wafted away from it. He did it again then put it in his mouth. "This is delicious."

She swallowed a spoonful. Not her best, but it worked from what they had on hand. Brodie's movements were getting slower. "Ye should lay down after ye eat. I'll tend to cleaning up and checking on the animals."

"'Tis cold out there."

Memories flashed of all the times her father had sent her outside to do the farm work, and Brodie had insisted she fill the water troughs while he did the more labor intensive tasks. Funny, she'd never realized before now how often he had willingly taken on those burdens for her, even showing up late in the day when he should have been at home resting after a hard day's work with his own family.

"The cold willnae hurt me." She gave him her best smile. "Ye can do it when ye get better."

"Nae," he insisted in a stern voice that belied his weak state. "I've worked out with one of the neighbors to see to the animals. I dinnae want ye out there until we ken what Ross and Argyll are up to."

Shuddering, she nodded. Being in her old home had given her a false sense of security—there were very dangerous men out there, looking for her. Rising, she grabbed the bowls to take them to the kitchen. "I'll stay in for now."

Only half of his stew had been eaten. When he'd been ill, her father had lost his appetite, too. Gut twisting at the thought, she put the dishes down without bothering to clean them and hurried back to Brodie's side.

As she strode into the room, she noticed he was shivering, so she felt his head again. His cheeks were too rosy and gave off heat as if he'd been standing too close to a fire.

"Let's get ye in bed." Taking his arm, she pulled him up.

"Do ye ken how many times I've wished to hear ye say that, and now that ye are here, I am as weak as a puppy."

"Ye'll be better tomorrow." She patted his shoulder and wished she hadn't, because her hand lingered. His muscles were firm and tight, and she envisioned him braced upon those arms above her as he made love to her. Her own cheeks warmed, and she turned from him to avoid his gaze as they walked down the hall.

"Will ye tell me to come to bed tomorrow?"

"I dinnae ken, Brodie. I find myself doing things I promised myself never to do again, and ye can believe that scares me."

Her rebellious body wanted him, and she wasn't sure she would be able to fight the attraction that had rekindled between them.

• • •

Brodie woke to a rumbling belly and a cold bed. Drifting in from the kitchen was a delicious aroma that beckoned him almost as much as the thought of seeing the angel who had apparently been cooking. It smelled so good.

Propping up on his elbows, he looked around. With the snow that still fell outside the window, it was impossible to pinpoint the time of day, but he knew Skye had been beside him at some point during the night, and she hadn't objected when he'd wrapped his arms around her and drawn her close to his chest.

Now, a dull light broke through the lingering storm. How had he slept so long? He threw the covers back and quickly dressed. Rubbing his eyes, he made his way to the kitchen, but not before looking out every window in the house to make sure the snow lay undisturbed, and that there were no signs of an imminent threat. As soon as the snow let them, he would have to get to Kentillie to make sure he had others guarding Skye as well.

Leaning on the doorframe, he enjoyed the sight of her in the kitchen, moving from task to task as if she'd never left. She'd changed over the years, but she was still that girl who jumped headlong into loving something with every fiber of who she was—a stray animal, cooking, and, at one time, him.

He found himself wishing for this life he could not have. The Royalist Raven needed to seduce Skye to do his job, but Brodie Cameron didn't think he could bring himself to do it. But how else to get the information he desperately needed?

"Good morning, bonny lass."

She turned, and her lips curved up. The smile was almost as lovely as the one she'd given Alan the day before, and he grinned. "How are ye this morning?"

"I feel normal again, thanks to yer care."

"Yer color is back." She put down the pot she'd been holding and sashayed over to him. Her hand rose up to meet his cheek, and he froze at the sensation her caress elicited. "Yer fever is gone as well. I think Maggie's medicine has done wonders."

"I think 'tis just ye being here." She started to pull her hand back, but he caught it and held it as he gazed deep into her green eyes. Tilting his head down as he pulled her tender flesh to his lips and kissed it. A sweet lingering touch. Her skin was as soft as he remembered, and his pulse quickened. She didn't pull away.

Slowly, he straightened, reluctant to take his lips from her.

"I have some breakfast ready." Her cheeks were pink, and she averted her eyes. Then she turned and broke his hold. She glanced over her shoulder as she started placing items he couldn't see on plates. "Go, sit. I will it bring to ye."

"I'll help."

"I may let ye do the cleaning. Looks like ye ken where everything belongs, unless ye havennae touched the kitchen since I left."

She turned back to her task, but he was glad she couldn't see his face when he confessed, "I tried to keep everything the same. It reminded me of ye."

At one time, he had held out hope she would return, and her delight made him glad he'd been so careful to keep everything the same. If she decided to stay, he'd give her back her home, and he would seek accommodations elsewhere.

"I forgot to tell ye, I sent a letter to yer uncle from the last inn to let him ken ye were safe and where to find ye. Do ye think he will leave me standing when he takes ye this time?"

The only real dealings he'd had with the MacDonald laird had been the day he'd overheard the conversation with Skye's father, the day the arse had called him a simple farmer, and after he had managed the treacherous passage to Alastair MacDonald's island to fetch Skye and bring her home. Her uncle had refused to let him see her, berated him for hurting her, and announced she'd be wed to another. Then, he'd given orders for men to escort him off the island. They had not been gentle in their removal of him, and he still ached at the memory of the beating he'd endured at their hands.

Which reminded him of his task—although he was certain she was innocent of conspiring with Covenanters, her uncle might not be.

"When yer uncle visited once, I found a Book of Common Prayer in yer house." It was a lie, but it was to make sure she was safe. If the MacDonald was conspiring with the man who would see his niece dead or worse, he wouldn't be returning her to the man. "Does he subscribe to the Covenants?"

One corner of her lips and brow turned up, and she seemed confused. "I'm surprised. I cannae imagine him having a copy. He would never give up his Catholic faith."

Her conviction went some way toward pacifying his concerns about the laird, but the man could be crafty enough to hide his true allegiance from those closest to him.

"He doesnae talk to me much about it, but as I told ye, he was in Stirling to form alliances. Mayhap I didn't say with other Royalist clans, but 'tis his purpose." Shrugging, she turned around, holding two heaping plates and started toward the other room, leaving him to follow. "Let's sit. I'm hungry."

His stomach rumbled at the buttery smell as he followed then took a seat at the table. Eggs, bread, and sliced meat filled the plate she positioned in front of him. It looked delicious. The steam still wafted off as he lifted a forkful to his lips and tasted. Och, if heaven wasn't just in having her here, it was her cooking.

"Ye arenae allowed to go back." She looked up sharply, and he laughed. "I will never survive if I'm left to cook on my own after this."

Her shoulders relaxed. "I am glad ye like it."

"Tell me more of yer uncle's plan. What clan does he wish to marry ye into?"

Her gaze clouded as if she were remembering something or someone. She blinked then said, "It doesnae matter. I dinnae wish to discuss who I'm going to wed, when I've been stuck with ye for days now. I dinnae think 'tis right."

"I would like to ken."

"'Tis no' fair to talk about him with ye when we have a shared past."

If she'd only answer the question, he could be certain her uncle was on the side of the Royalists. Maybe she *was* covering for him. The thought of her siding with the Covenanters stabbed at him. He'd become a spy because of the lessons her father had taught him—loyalty to God, clan, and the king. Those beliefs had been all that was left to him when she and her father had deserted him, and he had stayed his course with spying to honor his memory and teachings.

"Tell me more about yer uncle's island."

"There isnae much to tell."

"Do ye have many friends?"

"Aye, I have lots of cousins there, and since I was helping in the kitchens, I got to ken a lot of the people." Her eyes lit with excitement.

"I'm glad to ken ye were no' lonely. I will get ye over to see Donella as soon as we can leave."

She practically bounced in her seat, gracing him with that smile she'd given Alan. He would do what he could to keep it there with the limited amount of time he had left with her. "Aye, I have missed her terribly."

"And ye didnae miss me?" The words spilled from his lips before he could stop them.

Green gaze darting away, she visibly tensed. If he were smart, he would drop the subject. The last thing he wanted to do was put her wall back up.

"Why did ye tell Donella and Alan no' to let me ken how ye were?"

"I thought it would be easier on both of us that way."

"It was no' easy." He fought hard to keep the bitterness out of the words, but it did not work.

"Ye would never ken by the number of women ye have been with. It appeared to me that I was the last person ye were concerned with." She slammed her cup down on the table. Then picked up her plate, stood, and stomped toward the kitchen.

"What was I supposed to do? Ye left me. Then ye refused to see me. And within a few weeks were betrothed to another."

She set down her trencher and kept her back to him, her head dipping to stare at the plate in front of her. He could see she was wounded by his imagined indiscretions, a product of the double life she couldn't understand and he couldn't tell her. She would not be so resentful if she did not care for him, or maybe if she knew the truth of his spying and false persona.

He strode across the room in two long steps, took her by the shoulders, and gently turned her around. Her body was pinned between his and the wall. His head sank to hers, and the smell of lavender wafted up to his seeking nose. God, he loved the way she smelled.

She kept her gaze down, so he lifted his head and trailed his hand up her arm, across her neck and to her chin. Tilting her head back, he saw a single tear had escaped from her watering eyes. As it ran down her cheek, his heart lurched. He had not meant to make her cry.

"None of them meant anything. Do ye want to know why I was with those women?" She shook her head, but she had started this, and he was going to tell her the truth. "I was lost without ye. I had no purpose. Both ye and yer father were gone. Everything I had lived for since I was a lad of twelve was gone."

She bit her lip.

"I slept with those women to try to fill that hole. To feel like a person again. It never worked, and I stopped long ago. I needed ye, Skye."

He stroked her cheek, and she was silent as she focused her gaze directly on his. Something changed then, like she'd made some unspoken vow to herself, or as if she were reliving the past she had tried to wipe from her memory.

Suddenly her hand was on his cheek, gentle, searching. The caress mesmerized him, and he leaned into her.

"I have missed ye, too." Her words were so quiet that at first he thought he'd misunderstood.

Closing her eyes and sighing, she seemed to melt into his touch, as if the barrier she'd placed between them had vanished. Tunneling his fingers into her hair, he marveled at the soft, thick, blond strands sliding through his fingers, which awakened the part of him he'd thought he had locked away. Just as he had imagined over the years, just as he had remembered. He fisted the silvery strands as he leaned in to kiss her cheek. His temple rested on hers, and he smelled her honey and spice. Och, he had missed her.

When her eyes opened, she searched his, and this time it was without accusation of past crimes and misunderstandings.

Dipping his head, he put his lips to hers, asking for approval. Her mouth pressed harder against his, and every part of him came alive. He could not promise her a life together, but he could show her now how much she had meant to him.

He opened his mouth, and her tongue reached out, stroking for his, as everything disappeared and there was just her and him.

A blessed peace and contentment he'd not felt in five

years filled him, to be needed and wanted by the only woman who had ever held a place in his heart. She pulled back and gazed at him with emerald pools. "Take me to bed, Brodie Cameron."

A red-hot urgency assailed him, and he wasted not a precious second before he scooped her up in his arms, pivoted, and rushed toward the bedroom.

Chapter Eleven

Delicious chills tickled Skye's neck and ran through her spine as Brodie's fingertips trailed across her neckline and danced on her skin like the cool Scottish rains. His hand came to rest on the brooch holding the arisaid pinned to her fevered body. He raised his brow. It was a question. Was she sure? Was she ready to take this irrevocable step with him again?

She was sure he had been sincere. She was going to love him so hard that it would rip her heart out when she left, but he had always been the one. She might be betrothed now, but she was no fool—it was a marriage made of political alliances, and there was no love between Collin and her; there never would be. Her betrothed had said as much to her the night they'd met in Stirling.

She would be honest with the MacPherson laird's son before she went to their wedding bed, but if she didn't give in to this feeling, she would regret it the rest of her life and resent the husband she was hoping to be friends with. This would be her only chance to ever be loved and desired again, and she couldn't let it pass, because it would be the memories of these moments she would cling to on cold, lonely nights.

Brodie had apparently seen her hesitation because his finger leisurely teased her chest as he awaited confirmation. The sensation heated her blood and made her thoughts scatter. Tingles shot through her, and gooseflesh erupted on her arms, evaporating any second thoughts she was having of giving in to this overwhelming need to be one with him.

She brought her hands up to rest on his sides and looked deep into his dark chocolate eyes. "I want this, dearest."

"I want ye." He groaned, and his hand rose to clasp the back of her neck as his other arm wound around her waist and pulled her flush with his solid frame. He lowered his mouth to hers.

His lips were rough at first, like the first time they had kissed. She had never kissed another, and she was flattered by his impatience. Her hands tightened on his waist. He must have felt her response, because the kiss softened.

His tongue swept over hers and shattered any lingering resolve she possessed. She let her body melt into his as he continued his sweet, relentless assault, and her blood pounded as her core ignited. She was lost. Lost in the moment, lost in the passion, lost in the only man she had ever or would ever love. All rational thought of consequences had been wiped away with just his touch.

A small whimper escaped her as he pulled back to nip at her lower lip. He stilled and raised his head. The dark eyes looking back at her were intent, focused on her, and she felt herself drowning in the need they projected. She panted from her own sheer desire and longing. He shifted slightly, and his hard erection rubbed against her belly. Core heating, moisture pooled in her most intimate area.

"I've wanted for so long to have ye back in my arms." The deep, primitive tenor in his words resonated and called to the primal part of her she'd buried long ago. It started a thrumming in her blood that overpowered and shattered any sense of self-preservation she had been able to hold on to.

"Many a night I have dreamt of being here with ye." She did not recognize her own husky reply.

A hoarse rumble reverberated through his throat as he reached to deftly unpin her arisaid. At the same time, his head sank to her neck and his mouth landed just above her shoulder. A gasp escaped her as the warmth of his lips clasped around the sensitive skin. Shivers of heated awareness ran down the length of her body, spurring the need for him that she had kept locked away for far too long.

Her plaid fell to the ground as he tossed the brooch to a nearby table. The air in the room was cool, but her body heated as her hands traveled up Brodie's hips to unfasten his belt. Her fingers shook as she fumbled with it. He pulled away and grasped one of her hands. He placed it on his swollen penis.

"Feel what ye do to me, love." Heat pooled at her center as his strained voice and the proof of his need for her engulfed her with urgency. Letting go, he removed the belt easily, returning to lavish more attention on her collarbone, trailing kisses to her ear.

She slid her hands up his arms to remove the plaid from his taut body. She'd forgotten just how brawny and hard his biceps were as the steel beneath his velvet skin rippled under her fingertips. He bit down gently on the lobe of her ear just as the cloth fell in a soft lump to the floor.

As she arched into him, sparks raced to the apex of her legs. His hands snaked back around to rest on her rear, squeezed, and then lifted her to her toes as he ground into her with the proof of his desire.

Lowering her feet to the ground, he took a step back. His warmth was instantly missed, but the cold didn't jar her. What did was the look in his eyes as he watched her, the raw yearning as his hands untied the ribbons on her stays. He pulled at them as his gaze lingered on her chest.

"Yer breasts are larger than I remember."

Her cheeks reddened as his perusal lingered, and her stays fell to the ground as he reached up to gently palm a globe through her shift. Her already engorged nipples tightened as he reverently fingered one. An intense shot of desire coiled inside her.

His other hand skimmed along her thigh and up under her shift. She found it hard to breathe under his intent gaze and the sensations assailing her. A pinch at her nipple sent a shockwave that enveloped her in need as her womb tightened. His mouth turned up in a satisfied grin as his palm skidded across her feminine folds and felt the wetness there.

"Brodie," she whimpered. He seemed to understand her fevered need, because both hands lowered to the hem of her shift, grasped it, and pulled it up over her head in one fluid motion. It left her trembling body exposed to him.

Her heart raced as his hands rested on her hips and guided her to the solid bed. She sat and scooted back on her elbows as he yanked his white linen shirt over his broad shoulders. His muscles swelled, and she was mesmerized at how his body had transformed. He had been handsome before, but now, her mouth watered as she studied his solid, strapping chest. She was mesmerized as his muscles flexed and expanded when he tossed his shirt to the floor.

Trailing her gaze down to his penis, she swallowed hard and tried to control her stuttering breath. Even it was larger than she remembered as it stood erect, ready to fill her, and claim her once again.

She recalled their first time. It had hurt, but only at first because he had been gentle and had slowly given her time to adjust to his invasion. Would she need time to adjust again? He must have sensed her reticence because he said, "I willnae hurt ye, love. 'Twill be hard, but I will go slow. I want to savor every second I am inside ye."

She blushed at how easy he'd been able to read her. Nodding in relief, she admitted, "I have no' been with any other." Somehow, it was important to her that he know her heart and soul had remained faithful.

His lips curved up and both dimples flashed as his eyes dilated. When he slid onto the bed next to her, she scooted back farther to make room for him. The bed was small, and they just fit. He surprised her with, "I never brought another woman here. This is our place. I kept it that way."

"Why did ye stay in the smaller room?"

"This is where I had memories of ye." He turned on his side and rested on an elbow as he slid a finger across her hip then the curve of her waist. And she would have the memory of this moment when she needed it. Her eyes stung at the intensity and depth of emotion surging through her, and the knowledge that she would soon lose this again.

His lips covered hers, scattering the wayward thoughts like swirling leaves on a brisk fall day. She was enthralled as his tongue swept over hers and his exposed chest brushed against her breast, bringing a closeness she'd never thought to experience again. The feel of skin on skin ignited a fire deep inside her core. Although she had tried to deny it, she was lost to him.

As his mouth continued to devour hers, his hand slid down to cup her breast. It was gentle, but firm. He kneaded the soft flesh and groaned while she ran a hand through his thick locks and fisted the loose curls in the back. The kiss deepened, and his hand strayed down to gently tickle her ribs. It continued farther and rested on her mound as sparks cascaded through every part of her body.

His fingers played in her pubic hair, teasing the sensitive flesh hiding under her curls and tantalizing the feminine part of her that was ready to surrender to everything he offered. She arched up into his hand, and it slid into the folds to her wet channel. She gasped, and his head lifted to pin her with the intense proof of his need for her. "Ye are so wet for me, love."

She couldn't speak. She didn't have to; his hand eased down to grasp her thigh. Pushing her legs apart, he rose and repositioned himself over her. Bracing himself on one arm, he guided the tip of his manhood to her swollen core and ran it up and down the length, soaking up her juices and driving her mad. She whimpered with need.

Centering the head of his cock, he slowly slid into her. It didn't hurt, but she felt full and complete. He moved into her until she had taken in the whole length of him, filling and expanding her as he claimed her, heart, body, and soul. He took in a deep, strained breath then rocked his hips back and forth as she melted like clay in his hands.

"Skye, ye feel so good wrapped around me." The words ignited a primitive response inside her, and though he had stilled, she shimmied her hips back and forth, longing for the release that only he could give her.

His mouth came back down on hers, this time demanding and hard, challenging her to deny him, claiming her soul, her heart as his. Letting her know that he belonged to her completely, just as she did him. Just as she always had.

Brodie pulled out of her almost completely, stilled, and she immediately felt bereft as he tilted his head back to watch her. His gaze stayed on her eyes as he slowly slid back into her depths, burying his shaft inside her tight sheath, filling her to the hilt.

He swayed back and forth, not drawing back, staying buried deep inside her. The movement pushed his body over the sensitive nub at her center, and she inhaled as her eyes rolled back and a spasm spiraled through her body.

He moved his hips again. The head of his cock was buried deep inside her, stroking her insides as his body rubbed her on the outside. Her hands flew to his buttocks and held on as she arched further in to him, and he rocked again and again, over and over until a dam broke inside her.

Gasping for air as wave after wave of explosive fire ignited and spiraled through her, she succumbed to the sensations, and her senses spun out of control. It was a pleasure so intense it bordered on pain, and she clutched at his arms in a vain attempt to stay grounded as her world spun into a whirlpool of oblivion and ecstasy.

His rhythm changed, hips retreating and then plunging in an urgent plundering and claiming of her body. Her body was still clenching around his as the head of his cock reached the deepest part of her with a relentless hunger that thirsted to take everything she could give.

He sank into her over and over until his gaze locked on her. He was holding her head, watching her when his own release came. Rapture reached his eyes, and his seed pumped into her. Some primal part of her thrilled at knowing she had brought pleasure to him, driven him to the edge, and that her body had been made for his.

He thrust two more times as her channel continued to milk him, then he took her mouth again, fevered at first, then gentling to a soft, tender caress as if he worshipped her. It was so beautiful and so right.

Why had she denied herself all these years? And why had she not made things right between them when she'd had the chance?

She pushed away the voice that said, *Because ye would have ended up alone.*

• • •

Nestling into the apex where his arm and shoulder met, Skye relaxed as a small sigh of what passed for sated satisfaction escaped her throat. Brodie relished the silk of her next to him again, and the feel of pure contentment.

As she lay on her side in the crook of his arm, he trailed his fingers up and down her soft, feminine side, savoring every second of her nearness. She had been his first, but after she left him, he had spent many nights with others, trying to find what he had lost, the perfection that was Skye.

He never had. Nights with other women always left him feeling cold, hollow, and emptier than before. But now, this was all he could hope for, these few stolen moments, because he had chosen another path, and there was no going back.

"If ye missed me, why did ye no' come after me?" Her question startled him. He had thought her almost asleep.

"I did."

"When?"

"On yer eighteenth birthday. I came to marry ye and bring ye home. Yer father had said once ye were eighteen, we could wed."

"When did he say that?" She sat up and looked at him sideways.

"I asked him when ye were sixteen. We discussed it many times, but his answer was always the same."

"Ye came all the way to the Isle of Skye?" Her hands clasped over her bare chest, and her eyes narrowed.

"Aye. Did yer uncle no' tell ye?" Anger rose in his chest. The man had not even told her he had come and pleaded to see her.

"Nae, I didnae ken." Skye shook her head slightly.

"He said ye would no' see me."

"Well, I…" Her eyes darted away.

"Told me I wasnae good enough for ye, and he'd already made a match for ye and ye'd accepted it. He had me beat senseless."

"The first I heard of ye was that ye jumped right into bed with the next lass to come along."

"Nae, that came when I healed. After no one would tell me how ye were. And I asked. Donella, Alan, Lorna. They told me they had not heard from ye. I thought ye had deserted them, too. I drank so much whisky one night that I woke up in someone else's bed not kenning how I had come to be there."

Tears streamed down her cheeks. "I am so sorry."

He reached up to wipe away her tears, but she brushed his hand aside and dipped her head to kiss him. It was so tender, leaving him groaning.

"Ah, love, dinnae do that unless ye want me inside ye again. I cannae control myself when it comes to ye." She pulled back and gave him a mischievous grin then playfully nipped at his lower lip. A challenge. One he was more than ready to face.

Chapter Twelve

"Are ye no' hungry yet?" Skye rolled her eyes. How did Brodie have all this energy after his illness? All she wanted to do was eat and snuggle in his arms to fall asleep.

"Only for ye, love." He rose up above her and nibbled at her neck. She gasped and then sighed as the tingle spread through her veins. They had lain together twice, and he showed no signs of slowing.

"I'm famished," she pleaded, but craned to give him better access.

"Me, too. I've been starving for ye for far too long."

He climbed on top of her and, taking her hands, pinned them above her head. Her chest started to flutter, and she could feel the familiar longing for him, but her stomach growled in protest. This time it was loud enough to catch his attention. He frowned as he let go of her wrists, but stayed braced on top of her.

"We will have to continue later. It's getting dark, and we havenae left the bed all day," she said.

"I never want to leave this bed again, love." Grinding his

pelvis into her hips, he smiled wickedly.

"I promise we can come back. I just need food. Ye do, too, if ye'll admit it. Ye were just sick last night. Besides, I need to make ye Maggie's tea."

He groaned. "I dinnae like it. It's tastes like dirty water."

"If ye get sick again, ye willnae have the strength to make love to me," she countered with a wry smile.

"Ye win this one, but we will no' leave this house."

She laughed. "The snow wouldnae let us if we tried."

He rolled off her and kept his gaze fixed on her as she stood. She pulled her shift on quickly, not because of his scrutiny, but because she had not realized how cold it was. They had been warm all day in each other's arms under the blankets, and she was now second guessing her request to leave it.

"Will ye get the fire going while I figure out what to make?"

"Aye, anything for ye, lass." He rose, wrapping his plaid around his broad shoulders and walking over. Glancing out the window, he studied the scenery as if it was the first time he had seen it. Following her from the room, he stopped, moved into the spare bedroom, and glanced out that window, too.

She shivered—he was looking for threats. She was glad he was being vigilant, because she'd been so wrapped up in the pleasure of being with him, she'd forgotten about the men after her. Trusting him completely, she went to work in the kitchen.

Making a basic stew had been simple with potatoes she found in the cupboards and venison the Lochiel had left just outside in the cold. She added spices Maggie had sent and pulled out the bread that had been brought from the Kentillie kitchens. It was a perfect meal for two. Contentment washed over her as she realized cooking for just Brodie and herself had been calm and pleasant.

In the kitchen back on Skye, she had helped cook for a

horde of MacDonalds, and it was always bustling and hectic with no time to put care into the dishes she made. She had loved being lost in the flurry of faces and friends, but there was something magical about being in this place, just Brodie and her.

Here, she had time and could put all the care she wanted into the dish. Here, she didn't feel like just a cog in the wheel, which was what she'd wanted. Here, she felt important and needed.

Would she miss this?

Would she feel this way when she went to her new home? Would the MacPhersons even allow her to help in the kitchens?

Pushing the thoughts away, she decided to relish the sight of Brodie as he sat near the fire carving a piece of wood and peeking up at her from time to time.

After setting the stew, bread, and some ale down on the table, she slid into the chair next to his. She was amazed at how natural it felt and how relaxed she was in his presence. The comfortable ease they had shared as youths had come back so easily.

"How is yer family?" she asked.

"Mother and father are well. Tormod's family lives near them now. They have two babes and one more on the way. Kerk is always off somewhere. We dinnae see him much."

"Will they be pleased to see me?" Her eyes strayed out the window in the direction of his parents' home.

"I am certain they will be happy." He placed a comforting hand on hers and smiled. "I am surprised ye didnae come across them at Stirling.

"'Tis a large place. We arrived late, and then I was gone the same night. I do think I caught a glimpse of yer mother."

"Aye. They should return after the snow melts. Mayhap ye will see them before the MacDonald arrives." Concern flashed behind his eyes as his gaze turned and narrowed on the door. "'Twill also mean Ross and Neil could be here soon, and I havenae had the chance to find out what Argyll wants with ye."

"Oh." She still couldn't wrap her mind around what they wanted from her.

"Dinnae go out there without me until we ken where all the threats are coming from and why."

She nodded. She didn't want to find herself in the back of their wagon again, or worse yet, with Argyll, the man who was responsible for all those MacDonald women being pushed from the cliffs on Rathlin Island. A bone deep chill sped through her.

"We need to keep the door locked, too."

• • •

The steady drip of the melting snow set a rhythmic pace as Brodie lazily traced his fingers up and down Skye's arm. He did not mind that she still slept as he took the time to just enjoy her being there. The sun rose higher in the sky and was now shining in the window. A ray caressed her arm and hit a strand of her blond tresses that lay across the pillow, and he wished he could stop time.

But he couldn't, and it was time to get to Kentillie and make sure Lachlan knew of the threat to him and the clan chiefs at the meeting in Edinburgh, and also of Ross and Neil and the trouble between the MacLeans and MacDonalds. But the threat that concerned him the most was that Argyll was after Skye.

Stirring, she sighed, and he uttered a quick prayer of thanks he'd had this time with her. Her sleepy eyes fluttered open and came to rest on his. She'd had no practice seducing men, but the lazy, sultry look in those hooded green gems and the sinful smile she shot him hardened his cock instantly. Although his plan had been to get her to trust him, he was the one who had fallen, sucked in beyond hope like a boot in a muddy peat bog, no chance of ever coming out the same.

He had not taken her again last night. He had wanted to, but she was so tired and after yesterday, she might be sore. This morning, he wanted her. Leaning in, he claimed her lips, devouring their sweetness and sating his need to touch her.

Her hand grasped his side, and she arched into him, enticing him to take more as her breasts rubbed against him through her shift. The provocative move sent waves of need pulsing through him, which culminated in his hardening staff. It jerked in response.

His lips left hers, and between his labored breathing he was able to manage, "Love, I want to be inside ye. I am afraid I cannae wait."

Her mouth curved up as her eyes heated with approval. "Then take me." The words wrapped around him and pulled him further under her spell.

Half sitting, leaning on his elbow, he slid his arm around her waist and whisked her on top of him. She gasped, and her eyes widened. He couldn't help but grin at her response. They had been together a handful of times, but she had never been on top. It would be a new experience for her, and he was glad to be the one to teach her.

Her confession of the previous day had thrilled him—to know she'd never given herself to another, that he had been the only one to touch her and enjoy her wanton response. It galled him that once she went back to the Isle of Skye, her uncle would give her to the husband she wouldn't name, but he pushed the thought away to focus on this stolen moment.

"I want to watch ye above me as I enter ye. 'Twill give ye more control." She swallowed, and her cheeks reddened. "Do ye trust me, love?" She nodded. "Then, straddle me." She did.

"Now, take off yer shift," he ordered. "Nice and slow."

His heavy gaze studied her as she exposed her body to him. The taut skin of her abdomen, the soft curve up to her ribs, and the sway of her beautiful breasts enticed him as she shimmied the fabric over her head. She beckoned to him like a siren, just as she had always been able to pull him into the treacherous surf to be by her side.

She was up on her knees above him. He snaked his arm around her back as he moved to a seated position, his chest brushing hers. Leaning down, his mouth found one of her sensitive globes. He kissed her gently there and held her pinned with one hand at the base of her bare back.

He peeked up to see her mouth open, watching him, and he took her breast into his mouth and sucked at her nipple. She threw her head back and gasped. As she did, her slick center brushed against the base of his hardness and he fought the urge to grab her hips, lift her, then impale her as he sank into her tight sheath. His blood heated at her response, and he did it again.

This time when he pulled back, he laved the engorged peak, swirling his tongue in circles around the nipple. She whimpered, and her hips ground against his cock, and he knew he would not last long.

Her eyes returned to his; the desire in their dilated depths ignited a fire deep within him, a need he had never felt for another, only her. Her response to him seared him deep and branded him. He belonged to her completely.

"Ye keep looking at me and moving like that, love, and I'll spill my seed before I am even inside ye." He meant it. He had always been in control of his own body, but she did things to him no other woman could. With Skye, he felt like a rope pulled so tight he would snap.

Leaning back on one elbow, he trailed his other hand down her side, following her curves to the rounded globe of her rear. His hand slid forward and she shivered. He stroked down her thigh, up, then back down again. His fingers slid across her slick folds. Her breathing became heavy, and her lids fluttered shut as a small mewling noise escaped. She was so wet and ready to take him in.

One of his hands reached for the top of her hip while the other held his cock to guide her as he drew her down on top of him. He groaned as her slick folds engulfed him, sheathing him in her warmth. She was so tight, so right. He continued to guide her down until he was buried so deep inside her that they became one.

Her eyes were wide but excited. If he starting pumping into her, he would spill before she reached her peak. Being inside her was like being wrapped in a warm plaid on a cold night.

As he rotated his hips gently, she struggled to keep her focus on him. Stilling, he enjoyed the beauty of her above him. Her pale skin was rosy in the early morning rays, and her hair glowed with the beams that lit it like liquid silver. He reached up to touch the silken strands. It was the most beautiful sight he had ever seen.

She started moving. It was a slow exploration, and as the revolution of her hips rocked through him, he involuntarily arched into her. A pulsating need to drive into her almost made him lose control. She began a rhythm somewhere between tentative and urgent that threatened to keep him on the edge for eternity, just where he wanted to be.

After a moment of the sweet torture, she changed her pace, lifting and lowering her hips in a slow exploration. It was such delicious torment to watch her move above him as her swollen passage slid up and down on his cock. He gripped her thighs as she moved in and out, engulfing him with each return. He would not last long, and the desire to see her pleasure peak drove him to take charge, because her satisfaction had to come before his.

One of his hands reached toward her center, and his thumb came to rest on the nub at the apex of where they were joined. With each thrust down, he swiped it over her clit. She started making soft whimpering noises and lost her rhythm.

Feeling the first shudder as her womb clenched around him, he maintained his assault on her sweet spot as his hips rose and drove into her, faster and harder. She cried out as her climax came, and leaned down to brace her arms on either side of him as he continued to pound. Some guttural sound escaped from his own throat as his release came, his seed filling her as the contractions deep within her continued to constrict around him.

She collapsed on top of him. Her limp arms pulled in to hold his sides, and she was still, other than the rise and fall of her chest with her labored breathing. He savored the feel of her warm, sated body on top of his. Pushing back her hair, he kissed her temple. She sighed, satisfied and replete.

Later, as they lay there, sated, neither wanting to move, he trailed his fingers gently across her collarbone. Remembering he was the Raven, he came up on an elbow and met her gaze. He didn't want to ruin the moment, but at the same time, she deserved to know at least part of the truth. "I cannae promise ye a future."

He held his breath, waiting for a protest or angry response, but she surprised him with resignation, as if she already knew they would have to part. Her acknowledgment and easy acquiescence to his declaration saddened him more than uttering the words had.

"Aye, Brodie Cameron. I ken we are different people now."

Blocking all thought of what was to come, he spent the rest of the day pretending to be a normal man enjoying every moment with the love of his life.

Chapter Thirteen

When she woke the next morning, Skye was alone in the bed. Sun shone through the window, but it was faint, still early. She stretched then swirled the still-warm bedding over her shoulders before she got up to peek out the window.

Between the sun yesterday and the warmer air that had remained through the night, a good bit of the snow had kept up a steady drip during the night and melted enough that it was passable. The white that had blanketed the old pines and oaks had disappeared, and the sun glistened off the wet branches as the beauty of the familiar landscape washed over her. She soaked it in and tried to commit everything to memory. It would have to sustain her for a lifetime.

It had nearly ripped her heart in two yesterday when Brodie admitted he couldn't stay. She didn't know what held him back, but it was for the best. She had an obligation to the MacDonald clan and couldn't indulge the delusion that they could once again be happy. And she would never put herself in the position for Brodie to leave her alone and vulnerable again.

Turning her thoughts to today's visit to Kentillie, she took a calming breath. It had been so long since she'd seen her friends. Had they changed as much as she had?

"'Tis a beautiful sight," Brodie said as his warm arms closed around her from behind. She smiled and sank into the welcoming shelter of his body.

"Aye. 'Tis sad to see it go." She looked wistfully at the snow as it melted. It was a reminder their time together was almost done.

"Nae, I mean ye. I could never get enough of this view," his voice burred into her ear.

She smiled and leaned farther into him. "It feels like a dream. Too good to be true."

Brodie tightened his embrace and burrowed his head next to hers. "Come, love. Let's break our fast and get to Kentillie."

"Has it changed much?" She tightened her fists on the plaid and pulled it tighter around her while she let her thoughts drift to happy times and friends.

"Nae." He loosened his grip and turned her around to face him. Giving her a soft kiss on her forehead, he said, "Everything is pretty much the same. Ye ken about Donella's babe."

As girls, they had spent many a day planning their lives out together. Donella's dreams had come true. Hers had crashed like fragile pottery on stone.

• • •

The last few days with Skye had been more than Brodie had ever dreamed could be. Regret spiked through him. He had another day or two before he would have to face his lonely existence again.

Skye cut into his silent revelries. "Is something amiss?"

"Aye, love. I dinnae want to leave."

"Och, Brodie, I ken." Her free hand fisted on her chest over her heart, then she placed it over the same spot on him.

He opened the door and a rush of cold air blew in. As they stepped through the threshold hand in hand, his gaze drifted around to see that the melting snow was undisturbed and no threats were visible.

Skye continued to hold his hand as the door clicked behind them, and they strolled to retrieve the horse for the short journey to Kentillie. Once there, he could speak to Lachlan about protection around the cottage and Skye until he could clear the MacDonald and the laird could take her to safety.

As they neared the castle, the old oak where she'd first told him she loved him came into view, and he smiled. He drew the horse up short and jumped down, then reached up to take her hand.

"Come, love. Trust me. There is something I want to show ye." He squeezed her hand again, and she swung her leg around to slide into his waiting arms. The ice-topped, pearly white ground crunched under their feet as he drew her to the spot.

It was the sacred place where, on that long ago day, they had snuck away from her father's watchful eye. He still remembered the way her chest rose and fell from the exertion of the run and the thrill of finding a few moments alone unsupervised.

Her flushed cheeks had been beautiful, but the way she licked her lips as he took her hands in his had undone him. The feel of her soft body pushed against the trunk of the tree as he had pursued her there remained etched in his memory. He had carved their initials just days before she had left him.

He pointed. "I did this after the first time we made love."

Her jaw dropped as her gaze landed on the letters. Her

fingers traced the smooth etchings indented in the bark. "It looks as if it was always part of the tree." She took his hand, pulling it to her cheek. "I am sorry, Brodie. I am sorry for everything we lost."

He thought to pull her back toward "their" home and take her in his arms again, to never leave the shelter of her warm embrace, but the clan needed him and she deserved a normal life, not that of a spy's wife who would be in constant danger.

"Keep looking at me like that, lass, and we willnae make it to Kentillie today."

"Would that be so bad?"

Her eyes turned a darker shade of green, a combination of jade and deep emerald, sultry and hooded as they skimmed up and down his frame. His cock jerked in response to her gaze, coupled with the mischievous grin she shot him. Oh, he wanted so badly to turn her around and march her back into his bed.

He groaned and reluctantly pulled back. "Later. We will make time for that later. Let's get to Kentillie before ye destroy my resolve."

Chapter Fourteen

Brodie sat next to Skye on a bench at Kentillie castle, sides touching, hands linked under the table, taking advantage of every second together, as if even their bodies recognized that their time was short and they would soon part ways. Dim light from the cloud-covered midday sun filtered in through the windows as he peered down the table littered with drinks, bread, and cheese, and enjoyed watching his enthralled clan members while Maggie recounted the story of how she and Lachlan had met. Skye's jaw fell open, and she even gasped at times.

"'Tis so nice to have ye back, Skye," Elspeth said. His aunt, Lachlan's mother, had hugged Skye fiercely as they had entered the great hall. Elspeth had been friends with Skye's mother before she passed away, and had acted as a surrogate for Skye when she needed guidance.

"It feels like home. I have missed everyone." She swept her hands around in a gesture that encompassed everyone present.

"How is Alastair?" Elspeth asked as Brodie's gaze was

caught by Lachlan and Alan strolling into the hall, followed closely by Robbie, the secretive lad Lachlan had rescued from a traitor seeking to form alliances with Argyll. After extinguishing the threat to the boy, the Cameron laird and Alan had taken Robbie in, training him and making him one of the clan. Taking advantage of the melting snow, the men had gone to the village this morning on some urgent business.

Skye pivoted back to answer Elspeth as the men took seats near him. "My uncle is well, but I am fair certain he is beside himself with worry."

Skye recounted the tale of their journey. Just as she concluded the tale of the bandits they had encountered, Donella came rushing in, holding her newborn babe wrapped tightly near her chest.

"There ye are," Donella squealed as her eyes landed on Skye.

"Donella." Letting go of his hand, Skye jumped up and ran around the table. The two embraced, and a gaggle of jumbled words flew nonstop as the women talked.

With the women's attention diverted, Alan leaned in. "What were ye doing there in Stirling?"

"I was following Ross MacLean. I thought he might be behind the raids. When I found Skye in the wagon, I kenned I had to get her to safety."

"Ye should have been taking her to the MacDonald, no' bringing her here to take advantage of her."

Brodie stiffened.

Alan had no right to question him, when the arse had lied for years about continuing contact with Skye. He didn't know if he would ever be able to forgive the man he'd considered a friend.

"I dinnae trust that he isnae in league with the Covenanters." Brodie's jaw ticked but his eyes darted to Skye. The last thing he wanted was to go at Alan in front of her.

"Are ye mad?" Alan's eyes narrowed.

"He has no' once come to say he wishes to continue an alliance with us, and no one truly knows what he thinks over there on his secluded island."

"He would never betray his religion or the beliefs of his clan."

"Until we ken the truth, she stays here where she is safe."

"She is no' safe with the Raven."

Brodie's fists clenched again under the table.

"Enough, Alan." Lachlan growled. "Ye dinnae need to watch out for yer cousin. Brodie will do what's right by her, and ye damn well ken it, so stop being such an arse."

Thank God Lachlan had said something, because he'd come seconds from jumping over the table and pummeling Alan. His gaze swiveled back to the laird. "I sent word to the MacDonald that she is here."

"Aye. We'll prepare for his visit, then, and welcome him formally."

"There's more. I didnae figure what Ross is up to, but I was able to overhear a conversation about a plot to assassinate all the clan chiefs who are planning to go to the upcoming meeting in Edinburgh."

"Och. I was afraid the Covenanters were planning something." Lachlan rubbed his eyes then ran his fingers through his hair.

"And something else is going on. This business with the raids, 'tis no' just happening to Camerons. The MacLeans are falling victim to it as well, and they think the MacDonalds are behind it."

"Sounds like when the MacDonald arrives, we have more to discuss than just his niece." Lachlan rubbed his chin and leaned in.

Alan frowned. "There is no way Alastair is behind the raids on the MacLeans."

He nodded as Alan continued to defend his uncle. "I questioned Skye, and she believes him a staunch Royalist and Catholic."

"I've been telling ye all along. The MacDonald is no Covenanter." Alan shook his head.

"I'm starting to believe that true, but until we are certain, I willnae let Skye go with him. If he's starting a war, I dinnae want her anywhere near the man."

Lachlan interjected, "I've kenned Alastair a long time and dinnae think he would want to cause conflict. I was under the impression he wanted to form alliances. But until we are sure, keep yer eyes on her."

"That's no' the worst. The bandits who attacked us said Argyll wanted Skye and was offering a reward for her capture or death."

"What would Argyll want with her?"

"I dinnae ken. Do ye have some extra men ye can put around the cottage? I havenae seen anything, but I cannae be certain we arenae being watched."

"Done." Lachlan nodded. "The violence has escalated. We went to the village to retrieve Robbie this morning."

Robbie spoke for the first time. "I had gone to confession and was on my way back to Kentillie when a group of men rushed into the village with an injured boy."

Despite the several inches in height he'd gained in only the last few months, Robbie had a way of blending into the background and making one forget he was there. He seemed to go to confession a little too often for one who practiced with a sword like he would one day have to face down the devil himself. The boy had been raised by a priest, yet Brodie couldn't help but think the lad held secrets darker and more terrifying than his own. Maybe that was why Alan and Lachlan kept a close watch on him.

With a newly acquired deeper voice, Robbie shook his

head and blew out a breath before he began again. "The boy had been beaten and left for dead, but somehow managed to crawl out of the house to seek help. 'Twas the son of the blacksmith's apprentice and his wife."

Alan's jaw tightened. "The lad's only about ten summers. 'Twas their only child."

Swallowing, Robbie shook his head as storm clouds raged in his gaze. "The boy's parents didnae survive."

"Did the lad tell ye what happened?" Closing his eyes, Brodie prayed the boy would not blame himself for what had happened, as he somehow knew Robbie blamed himself for the death of his previous guardian.

"Nae, he is in nae shape to talk." Robbie's eyes darkened further.

Lachlan continued, "We went to the village to bring the lad up to Coira, but I think Maggie should take a look at him, too." His head dipped toward Skye. "As soon as I see Maggie to the sickroom, I'll send a messenger to make sure yer letter made it through the snow to the MacDonald, and we'll put some guards around yer house until Skye's safe."

Scraping his chair across the floor, Lachlan rose to leave. Robbie followed, Alan trailing them, concern etched on his features. Skye's cousin had been an orphan, his parents dying in a fire when Alan was young. Maybe worry over the lad's condition explained why Alan had been so harsh with Brodie about Skye.

Returning his gaze to her, he attempted to shake the tensions that were plaguing the clan as he stood to walk toward the ladies. Elspeth handed Donella's babe to him to hold, and he took the little bundle and smiled down at him.

"Greetings, wee one," he said as he made little cooing noises and its tiny hand clasped his finger.

Smiling, he glanced over to see Skye had gone pale. Her eyes had glossed over with ghosts he couldn't name, and she seemed to be looking straight through him. He turned to look, but there was no one behind him. She staggered and almost fell over.

"Skye," Elspeth said as she steadied her with a sure hand.

"I am so sorry. I think 'tis all too overwhelming. I need to step outside for some air." She left before any of the ladies could protest. Their gazes followed her with concern as she made her way out the door.

He carefully placed the babe back in Donella's arms then hurried after her.

He found her slumped over on a bench just outside the door. She was a picture of sadness and loss that twisted his gut.

Easing down beside her, he reached out and rubbed her back. She flinched at first, but then softened to his touch as she buried her face in his shoulder.

"Skye," he whispered. When she didn't respond, he gently took her chin in his hand. "Look at me," he said with more force. "What has happened, love?"

She bit her lip and gave him the weakest smile he'd ever seen. "I lost…" Tears streamed down her face. "Our babe. I was with child when I left. It didnae survive." She hiccupped.

He sat frozen. She had been pregnant with his bairn, and the babe hadn't survived. But he'd come to Skye to get her not long after she'd left, and they had only been together a few times before then.

Why would her uncle have refused him? Why did the arse not force him to take her as his wife? Instead, the man had him beaten and sent him away. If he had tried again, would the MacDonald have let him claim her, knowing she had carried his bairn? Would things have been different if he'd gone back for her one more time?

"What?" was the only response he could muster. He pulled her onto his lap and sheltered her with his arms wrapped around her waist. She took a determined breath. Her face was right in front of his, but she appeared to be somewhere else when she started speaking in a resigned voice. The tone belied the pain he had just seen in her eyes.

"Just before my birthday." She blinked then resumed her unfocused stare. "My back hurt so badly. It felt like someone had stabbed me with a knife and twisted. Then there was so much blood. I had just realized I carried yer babe, and I was happy. That must be why Uncle had ye beaten. I lost the babe before ye arrived. I was so alone, and I hadnae told anyone, but the healer figured it out."

"It happens. 'Twas no' yer doing."

"I cried for days, and the healer told my uncle what had happened. He had already arranged for me to wed a MacLeod, but my state threatened the union, and he must have blamed ye."

The beating he'd endured at the MacDonald's command made sense now. He was surprised the man hadn't had him killed.

"I saw ye with Donella's babe, and it made me think of what we should have had."

He drew her close and buried his head in her hair at the way his life had been taken from him—Darach, Skye, and now their child. To hell with his pride, he wanted to roar his fury. For her, for him, for the baby they'd lost and the life they should have had. To know she'd gone through that without him to hold her tore at him with sharp talons of regret.

He'd give anything to take the hurt away from her, to turn back time and change everything. He would have found a way to get to her, if he'd only known.

They embraced and consoled each other for what felt like hours, then he finally pulled back. "There was nothing ye could have done."

"Mayhap if I hadn't left. I was so alone. I barely kenned

my cousins and uncle at the time."

"Nae, dinnae even think it. Ye ken that is why my brothers are so much older than me. My mother lost three babes. 'Twas no' ye."

"The MacLeod no longer wanted me when he found out." The admission left him cold and bitter. The man couldn't have ever met her, because no man on earth would be so stupid as to let her get away. "It's one of the reasons I cannae stay. Ye deserve a family, and I willnae be able to give ye what ye need. And, ye were always gone. I cannae be alone again."

He ached. He wanted to say it didn't matter, that he didn't need a family as long as he had her, but he couldn't. He wanted to say if she stayed she'd never be alone again, but he was the Raven.

"Come. 'Tis cold. Let's tell Donella ye are tired from the strain of caring for me the last few days and go back to the house."

· · ·

Skye woke to the most delicious tingles pulsating through her humming nerves. Skilled fingertips danced across her belly, circling her abdomen and teasing her ribs. She opened her eyes to see Brodie's sensual dark gaze focused on her. She started to protest and sit up, but the hand on her flattened and held her in place.

"Brodie," she tried to object, but his name escaped in a throaty whisper that was anything but stern.

He gave her a devilish grin. "I just want to touch ye, love."

His fingers glided up to her ribs. It tickled but at the same time sent shivers racing through her. At some point during the night, her shift had slid up around her waist and his hand had glided under it.

"I only want to see yer pleasure." He leaned over her, his

mouth so close to her neck that warm air teased her tender skin and set every part of her body ablaze.

Her mouth went dry. She licked her lips then bit down on the lower one, swallowing the protest she meant to utter. Mesmerizing eyes watched her so intently she might go up in flames from the intensity of the desire as he willed her to give in.

His fingers dipped lower to graze the curls at the apex of her legs. His hand slid down and back up, and she moved into his touch. Fire danced in her core as he played with her hair, gliding around the base then slightly pulling and teasing the curly strands.

She gasped as one side of his mouth tilted upward in a wry, knowing grin that melted her insides and captivated her gaze. His hand dipped farther, trailing down her thigh, leaving tingles of need in its wake. Grasping her knee, his hand pulled her legs apart and pinned the one closest to him between his warm, demanding thighs, spreading her and giving him access to that most intimate part of her.

Suddenly, his lips were on her nape, sending sinfully delicious spirals of desire to her core. She groaned and involuntarily tilted into him. His teeth bit down, and his soft lips ringed flesh as he sucked just where her neck met her shoulder. A primal groan of pure need escaped her lips at the feeling.

His fingers started working again, running up and down her thigh as he continued to worship her neck with his mouth. The overwhelming sensations were driving her mad with desire, and her core heated as moisture pooled in her most private of parts. One finger trailed slowly up her slick folds to skim across her clitoris, and he groaned.

His head slanted up to her ear, and his warm breath heated her blood as he whispered, "Ye are so wet for me, love."

Before she could think about what he had said or how to react, his finger had sunk back into her folds, trailing up and down as he teased her swollen nub with each stroke. His gaze pinned her with such need, she almost drowned in it.

One thick finger plunged into her tight sheath, and she squirmed at the delicious invasion. Her breath caught and she froze, but his tongue swept around hers again, and she was lost. Returning the kiss, she was barely aware that her hips rose up to beg for more.

Stroking the inside of her channel with slow, deliberate fervor, his ministrations almost pulled her under. Drawing back, he inserted a second finger that filled her until she thought she would burst. She felt a contraction in her core as the pressure of his thrusting fingers drew her closer to the edge.

His thumb started circling her nub as the plunging deepened and changed to a deliciously deliberate pace. His head tilted back to gaze at her, and she was caught in the intensity. His eyes were primitive as they studied her, claiming her with a dark, primal desire she knew must be reflected in her own eyes.

Her fists tightened on the bedding as a coiling tension raced through her, taking her to the apex, ready to burst. She broke as tremors raced through her body.

"Brodie," she gasped as her head tilted back but her eyes stayed fixed on his as her muscles tightened and clenched around his fingers. Cries of pleasure escaped her lips as she panted with the release. Wave after wave of ecstasy washed over her.

Her sheath was still spasming when his mouth returned to hers, hungry and needy, taking her cries of pleasure and demanding her soul.

It felt so right. She gave. She kissed him back with all the need, desire, and love she had kept hidden away. She could not deny he had conquered her. Again. She was lost to him. Lost, and her heart soared at the completion. Lost, and it scared her.

Withdrawing his hand, he tossed his arm over her and drew her closer to his side. Still trembling from the aftershocks, she lay there in his embrace. His erection was pressed up to her thigh as his leg remained coiled around hers, but he made no move to further their connection. He only held her. She felt cherished, as if she were the only woman in the world.

She shifted, climbing on top of him and when he entered her, they made love slowly, savoring each second as if they could make up for all the time they'd missed.

After they were sated, they lay together, glowing and relaxed. She couldn't remember ever feeling so complete. Brodie knew the truth about the babe and didn't appear to be angry or disgusted with her, and there was a closeness between them that had been missing before.

It was like the pieces to her broken heart had been put back together. But she would be a MacPherson soon, and he would go back to living here in her home without her.

Snuggling deeper into the space between Brodie's chest and arm as his fingers slowly danced up and down her arm was heavenly. She had almost fallen asleep when he spoke.

"What do ye think the MacDonald will do when he catches up to us?"

"He will thank ye for saving me from my captors, although he might be a bit angry ye didnae take me back to Stirling right away."

She felt her mouth turn up as she thought of the uncle who had gone out of his way to make her happy. After they arrived at Cairntay, he had said she reminded him of a caged bird who had lost her music. And she had been, for a while, pinned in by pain that kept her from thinking about returning home. Since the broken betrothal, he'd not asked anything of her until now. She'd finally moved on, throwing herself into the kitchens and her family, determining that she would never find herself alone when she needed someone again. That was why she had to marry Collin—he lived in a large castle full of family and friends. Even if she told him she loved another, and he released her from their betrothal, she couldn't trust that she wouldn't end up alone in this house waiting for Brodie to come home. She would never be able to take the loneliness.

Brodie broke into her thoughts. "I dinnae believe he will be so pleased to find ye here with me. He has years of anger built up towards me. Or mayhap he didnae mean it when he said, 'If I see yer face again, I will tear ye apart with my own hands.'"

He laughed it off, but a bone deep shiver ran through her as she recalled the last man her uncle had made that threat to, the very man that hunted her now—the Earl of Argyll.

Chapter Fifteen

The sun peeking through the curtains to signal the new day, birds chirping in the tree just outside the bedroom window, pulled Skye from a peaceful sleep. Stretching, she glanced over to see Brodie awake, but his gaze was fastened on the window, not her, his forehead creased with worry. His muscles were tense, and his boyish charm had been replaced by the steadfast resolve of a warrior.

She stiffened. "Do ye see something outside?"

"Nae. All looks well. We should just keep our guard up." But his casually dismissive tone made the hair on her arms stand up, and she surmised that something had raised his suspicions and he was attempting to soften her concern. He was not the kind to bring up an unfounded fear.

"Ross has no' yet made an appearance. He doesnae give in easily, especially if I am involved. We have a bit of a history. But what worries me more are Argyll's orders."

"Did ye talk to Lachlan? Had he seen them or heard anything?" She was surprised at how easily the man who had kidnapped her in Stirling and the Covenanter earl had slipped from her mind. She had been so focused on Brodie being ill, and then on savoring every moment they had left together, that she'd pushed all else to the back of her mind.

"Nae, he has not. But that doesnae mean the threats arenae nearby. Ross is a crafty bastard, and Argyll has men everywhere." The lines on Brodie's brow deepened.

"Mayhap they gave up and went home. It's been too cold to skulk around looking for me."

"I heard some odd noises last night. 'Twas probably nothing, but we should be vigilant. Lachlan has assigned men to keep watch over the house until the MacDonald arrives, but ye can never be too careful. Do ye have a dog on the Isle of Skye? They sense danger before people can."

"Nae, dogs are too much work. Truthfully, I have always wanted a cat." Despite the sincerity to her words, she couldn't help but smile inwardly at what she knew his reaction would be.

He scowled, and a satisfied smirk spread across her lips. Brodie had never liked cats. Once when they had been at Donella's, Skye had picked up a wee baby kitten and tried to get him to hold it. He had backed from the room and disappeared. Since then, she'd teased him about his aversion to the small animals that she found warm and comforting.

"What do ye want one of those creatures for? Their claws are vicious, and they smell." He shuddered and she laughed.

"The wee things are irresistible."

"Ye are irresistible." He rolled on top of her and tickled her. She laughed, and her bare body rubbed against his, reigniting the fire for him that burned deep and hot.

• • •

After spending the morning visiting with Brodie's mother and father, Skye found herself sprawled on the floor of his parent's stables inspecting a new litter of puppies. She giggled as a scruffy little collie with deep soulful eyes jumped into her lap. The others rolled and tumbled as they played and yapped. Nipping at each other, they rustled the hay, kicking up a slightly earthy mildew smell.

The only pup that had stopped to investigate her wore black and white on its face like a mask. It pounced up and stretched its paws onto her chest, and its silky black nose pressed into her neck before it licked under her chin.

"He likes ye." Brodie's deep voice sent chills through her as he knelt behind her, his face so close she could almost feel his breath on her neck.

The pup licked again, and she pulled back, right into Brodie's hard body. It was warm and solid, reassuring. Turning into him, she was met by his warm brown gaze. He took a lock of her hair and twirled it around his finger.

"Brodie."

"Aye, love." His lazy, hooded gaze heated her as her breath became shallow, and she suddenly didn't want the moment to end, didn't want her uncle to come for her. This was the life she was meant to have.

Was there any way to bring it back? Was there any way her uncle could or would release her from her obligation? Would she face the chance of being alone for just a little more time with Brodie?

"Kiss me." Licking her lips, she inched closer to his warmth, determined to enjoy every second she had left with him. Her hand slid under his plaid and inched higher, caressing his leg and eliciting a soft moan from deep in his throat.

Brodie's fingers forked through her hair to grasp the back of her head. Pulling her in, he said, "Ye are going to drive me mad, love." Then his lips were crushing hers.

He tasted of sweet honey and wine, of the promise of

more to come. This was where she belonged, in his arms, with the man who had always held her heart in the palm of his hand. But it might destroy her if she stayed.

A soft scratching on her arms startled her. She pulled back to see the rest of the pups had stopped playing with each other and were now bouncing around them looking for attention.

"Och, love." He took a deep breath and shook his head. "I was about to take ye on the stable floor. I think 'tis time we get back. I'll go tell Mother that we'll come back for the late meal."

"Aye, dearest. I want ye in my bed." She gave him what she hoped was a *take me there and ye will not regret it* look. She must have succeeded because his eyes dilated, and he pinned her with such a hungry gaze that she thought he would lay her down and finish what they'd just started.

He stood and turned to walk from the small space as she leaned back on her palms to watch him leave. His muscular legs were at eye level, and she could almost feel the silky steel of them rubbing with hers as they lay tangled together.

She sat up then cradled the pup in her arms and stood to watch his powerful legs carry him toward his parents' home. A chill breeze blew through the stable. She shivered. The snow had melted out in the open, but patches of the white stuff remained in shaded areas, and a bitter cold had moved back in.

Scampering around the corner, a dark haired boy who looked to be all of about four years appeared. His inquisitive eyes landed on Brodie, then he squealed and ran toward him. Brodie picked up the smiling child and twirled him around in circles. The wee one smiled up at him with matching dimples.

Skye's heart started to thud. The slant of his nose and the slightly larger tip at the end were identical to Brodie's. It struck her like a blow to the chest when she had a flashback of Brodie as a child. The lad could have been Brodie's twin. Nora Stewart appeared from around the corner of the house holding a babe, and Skye realized these were his brother's children.

Brodie's head dipped as he lovingly smiled and placed a kiss on the wee babe's head. Her heart stilled, but at the same time, it beat out of control. Erratic, irrational, terrified.

Her gaze locked on the boy still in his arms. Brodie's face glowed with the love he held for his nephew—the one thing she wanted so desperately to give him and knew she couldn't. A strange resignation flooded her senses—she had been wrong. She didn't belong here. She couldn't give Brodie the family he deserved, and she couldn't stand the heartbreak of not having a family to keep her company when he left her alone.

With numb arms, she lowered the puppy to the ground. It peeked through heavy lids and yawned, but went right back to sleep as she laid it tenderly with its siblings. They had curled up in the straw and stilled. At the loss of its warmth she shuddered again. It belonged here, warm and safe with its family. She had no family here.

The small space had become stifling. She needed air, but didn't want them to see her, so she pivoted and walked in a disoriented haze to the door at the back of the stables. The air wasn't enough to give her the clarity she sought.

Heavy feet carried her toward her old home. Breathing became difficult as each inhalation became lodged in her throat, and no matter how she tried, her lungs would not fill. It felt as if a heavy object pressed against her chest, crushing her along with any dreams she harbored that she and Brodie might still stand a chance.

It was for the best. She should be happy knowing that once she left he would be able to find a woman and have the family he dreamed of. After all, it was what she should wish for him as she moved on to take her place with the MacPherson clan.

Chapter Sixteen

Following Skye back toward the house, Brodie wondered what had caused her to walk off, shoulders down as if she had just lost a battle. Her gait was slow and measured, so he'd almost caught her by the time she reached the cottage. Why had she not waited on him?

A snap sounded from the nearby trees. His gaze was pulled in that direction as the implications of her actions washed over him. She would be an easy target for Ross or any of Argyll's men if she weren't paying attention to her surroundings. And what would happen if someone discovered who he was and came after her to get to him?

Had he been discovered? Hell. What if that was the reason Argyll was after her?

He caught a glimpse of her walking inside and shutting the door behind her, so he scanned the woods again and then ran the rest of the way to the cottage, intending to give her a piece of his mind for being so careless.

He found her in her room, a satchel in her hand, tossing in a couple of gowns that Maggie had given her. "What are ye doing?"

"I'm going to Kentillie."

"Why?"

"Ye dinnae need me here. I'm just a reminder of what can't be."

"Nae, ye cannae leave. Argyll and Ross are still out there. Have ye forgotten about them?"

"I havenae. Alan can see me home. He'll keep me safe."

"I can keep ye safe." He stepped closer, trying to bridge the distance that was suddenly between them.

"But 'tis no' fair. Ye need to find someone else and have a family."

"I dinnae want anyone else."

"But ye dinnae want me, either, and I must marry another."

She couldn't leave until he had answers.

"Ye cannae go back to the MacDonald. What if he is in league with Argyll?" Taking the bag from her hands, he tossed it onto the other side of the bed. It slid off and made a soft *thunk* as it hit the floor.

"That's insane."

"Stay with me a little longer. Just until I ken the truth." His arm snaked around her waist, and his lips crashed down on her neck. He had to keep her here.

She pushed him away. "Are ye using me to play some sick game with my uncle? Did ye sleep with me to get back at him by ruining my marriage possibilities?"

"Nae." But apparently she'd seen something she didn't like, because she shoved past him and walked out toward the main room.

He was the only one who could protect her. No one else would be as vigilant. The danger she was in had frayed every nerve in his body. Yet, if she stayed, his situation would put her in more jeopardy.

Suddenly, the knowledge that she would be walking out of his life again became real, and it killed him. Could he risk asking her to stay? Find a way to keep her here with him? Was there any way out of this life he'd created?

But he knew the answer to that—maybe she was better off in Kentillie.

· · ·

"I willnae let ye use me to get to my uncle." Skye shook her head just as Brodie's hand clasped hers.

"Nae, I amnae trying to hurt him."

"Ye have never been good at lying to me, Brodie Cameron." She tried to pull her hand free, but he held fast, looking at her as he had when she'd questioned him about his disappearances in the past. "Ye want to ken why I never came back? Ye were always gone and would lie about where ye were when I asked ye."

She took a steadying breath and let her gaze slide to his as the heartache played over again in her head. "Then ye left me alone, wondering where ye were, wondering if ye would come back."

A chill washed over her, and she shoved at him, attempting to put distance between them, but he tightened his hold, pulling her in, coiling his arms around her waist. "Father was terribly ill and ye left. I was so exhausted. I'd been trying to nurse him to health for days. I had no one when he died. I cried for hours, holding his hand, scared and alone, before I was able to get the strength to go find Alan."

Her thoughts jumped to the death of her mother, the baby foxes, her father, and then finally that of her babe while she'd been dropped off at Cairntay amongst people she didn't know and had locked herself away. She remembered again why she couldn't stay and why she had to go to the MacPhersons.

She could never face another death alone.

This time when she pushed, his arms loosened and fell to his sides. She moved to the window, staring out, not able to meet his gaze. "Every time you disappear, someone dies, and then ye are nowhere to be found."

Turning to look him in the eyes, she continued, "I couldnae trust ye to be here."

"Stay there. I'll be right back." He turned and walked away.

Chapter Seventeen

Brodie rushed toward Skye's old room. Knowing the truth now, understanding why she had left him without a word, his heart ached at all they'd lost because of his quest to uncover the truth about her uncle, his quest to redeem himself, because of fate.

From the cabinet in the corner of the room, he picked up a small, unassuming jar from the bottom shelf, removed the lid, and tipped the contents into his hand. He fingered the golden bands that still looked as shiny as they had the day he'd bought the ring. He had known then she would love it, but now he wondered if it was cursed.

He'd bought it on one of his first missions, a trip he'd made to England with Lachlan and his cousin's father before the previous laird had passed, the very same journey on which Lachlan's father and he had put together the plan for him to start spying for the Clan Cameron and the Royalist cause. He had held onto the jewelry all these years.

The shopkeeper had told him it was called a gimmel ring, and he'd been immediately drawn to it, using all the coin he'd brought with him, plus what his uncle had lent him, in order to purchase it for Skye.

Images flashed in his head as he remembered the day he'd taken it out of its special hiding place to show Nora. She had just agreed to marry his eldest brother and he already considered her a sister. Wanting to get her advice on the best way to ask Skye to be his wife, he had rushed outside to show her.

When he finally thought he had the right approach, and was about to go to ask Skye to marry him, Alexander Gordon had appeared at his house and requested his help on a mission in Inverness. He'd had no opportunity to tell anyone where they were going or even that he was leaving.

The last thing he'd expected when he returned was to find Darach dead and Skye gone. He could show her now that he had loved her, explain to her that she had been the only one for him. But he couldn't go back in time to be with her at her father's death or during the loss of their child, nor could he promise to be there for her in the future.

She'd lost faith in him. He could never explain his absences, couldn't turn back time, but maybe if he showed her this ring, she would understand how much she had meant to him.

A need to know whom she was to wed assailed him. Would the man be a Royalist and be able to keep her safe? And what if she now carried his babe? Could he live with another man raising his child?

• • •

When he reappeared, Brodie's dimpled smile lit his cheeks. "On one of those trips, I bought this for ye."

His gaze drifted down as his nimble fingers showed Skye what he had apparently retrieved from her old room. Gold glinted as a ray of sun peeking in the window hit the small object. "I've held onto this for such a long time." He pinched the base of a small ring and brought it up for her inspection. "When I found this, it made me think of us."

Small, intricately carved hands clasped each other in a sweet embrace. It was lovely and looked delicate in his grasp. He deftly pulled part of the ring apart to reveal a separate ring. A beautiful red stone carved in the shape of a heart had been hidden beneath.

One hand covered her mouth while her other went to his palm. She gently fingered the stone and cool metal. She'd never seen anything like it.

"I still cannae give you all the answers ye want, but ye should ken, ye always had my heart, Skye."

Fluttering started in her chest.

His hand took hers, and he held it. His gaze was locked on hers, and he peered so deep inside her that the last of her defenses crumbled as all the ill feelings she had harbored over the years evaporated. She licked her lips, then her teeth nipped down on the corner of her mouth.

"I saved it, hoping to be able to do this one day." His thumb grazed back and forth over her knuckles, and tingles of awareness raced straight to her heart. He let go and put the pieces of the ring back together before taking her hand again.

In his gaze, she saw a need so stark and sad that it called to the most primitive part of her being.

"'Tis beautiful." She breathed the words out almost like a whisper.

He held the bands to her finger. "I cannae offer ye a future or undo what has been done, but this belongs to ye. It always has."

The cool metal slipped on smoothly, and his hand lingered on hers as he studied it on her finger.

"Please stay until yer uncle comes. I promise nae to leave

ye alone."

She nodded.

Clearing his throat as if something had become lodged in it, he suddenly shifted, turning his back to her and acting as if the moment hadn't just happened. "I'll put more peat on the fire. 'Tis time for the midday meal. I told Mother we could come back for the late one."

Then he walked from the room, leaving her to wonder why, despite the feelings she knew he still held for her, he would not be willing to take her back. But she had an obligation as well, and it was best not to linger over what could have been.

· · ·

The MacDonald had not shown, and Brodie found himself stabling his horse to make his way to the nearby tavern for a prearranged meeting with the leader of the Royalist Resistance. His thoughts kept drifting to Skye, alone at the cottage with only the many extra guards posted in strategic locations around the property reassuring him she was safe.

Unfortunately, there was no way he could miss this meeting—he had too much vital information to offer, and was hoping to get answers, too.

His informant lounged at a table looking more deadly than any other man he knew. Alexander Gordon was not a man to trifle with. Part of the Gordon clan had sided with Royalists, and the other side, Covenanters, but Alex had gone his own way and forged a band of warriors, militia men, and, of course, Isobel McLean.

Giving the nearest tavern wench a wink as he shuffled to the table next to Alex's, he used his best unsteady voice to call out, "A drink lass," as he plopped down in the chair with his back to the Rebel leaders.

"Yer late," Alex clipped.

"And I cannae stay long," he muttered over his shoulder as he used his hand to block the movement of his lips. Motion caught his attention, and his gaze was pulled to the approaching barmaid.

"Pleasure to see ye, Brodie," the tavern wench purred as she came to stand in front of him. "If ye willnae pass out on me this time, we can head to a room in the back." She plied him with a seductive smile as she set an ale down in front of him.

Returning a provocative glance, he answered, "Now, I dinnae believe I would ever let a drink keep me from yer arms, Becca." Her father came out of the back and called for her, probably to keep the pretty maiden from succumbing to his charms.

"I dinnae ken how ye turn that on and off." Was that a hint of amusement he heard from the man behind him?

"It takes practice. Now do ye have any news for me? We have to make this quick."

"There is definitely an attack planned in Edinburgh, but the only names I've been able to get are Niall Campbell and Hamish Menzies. Ye will have to be certain someone is watching them."

"I'll look into them. I have news for ye, too. When I was in Stirling, I heard rumors that Isobel's identity has been compromised." Becca was watching him again, so he saluted her with his cup and made a show of spilling a portion of the contents on the table.

"She says someone has been attacking MacLeans," Argyll's most wanted drawled casually, but Brodie sensed a bite in the man's tone.

"I heard that. The Camerons have had some incidents as well."

"Who do ye think is behind it?"

"I dinnae have enough information to make a guess." He held back his suspicion that the MacDonald was behind the attacks. He asked the question that was eating at him, despite the desire to keep her name out of it. But Alexander might be the only way to learn what he needed. "I've heard Argyll has men out looking for the MacDonald's niece. Have ye heard anything?"

"I've heard, but no' why. That does no' bode well for the lass."

Och, he needed to get back to her—although he trusted Lachlan's men, no one could protect her the way he would.

"I have to go."

"Same time, a week from today?"

"Aye." He stood and stumbled toward the door.

Just as he was reaching the exit, he heard Becca call behind him, "Brodie, come back." But he was already out the door.

He was staggering back to the stable so he could rush back to Skye when the very faint scent of smoke—wood, not peat—hit him through a chill breeze from the east.

Skye. Instinct hammered him that it had something to do with her.

As fast as possible without raising suspicion, Brodie mounted and guided his horse out of the stable, then he thundered off. The closer he got to his home, the thicker the scent, and the fiercer his head pounded. The short ride from the village seemed to stretch as his mind filled with horrors, and he wondered if Argyll's men had found Skye and set the cottage on fire as a warning that none should cross the Covenanters.

He raced across the frozen farmland and was relieved when the structures came into view. All seemed unharmed, although a haze hung low over the buildings. A group of Lachlan's men—those charged with guarding Skye—hailed him as he approached, and he relaxed, the tension in his muscles easing. Maybe one of the outlying sheds on a nearby farm had sparked, because if there were still a dangerous blaze, the men would be busy containing it, instead of gathered around his home.

Once Brodie dismounted, a few of the men told him about a fire they'd doused at the edge of his property. Probably a few Cameron lads had been careless, become chilled while foraging or looking for game, and set a small fire for warmth. It appeared the lads had tried to smother the flames with a wet old plaid, which was what had produced all the smoke. After the guards had extinguished the small blaze, they gathered back at the cottage to share a dram before spreading out again to keep watch.

Aye, some of the little ones were careless, but the men's explanation didn't set right with Brodie, and he glanced at the cottage. Suspicion gnawed at him. "And Skye?" he asked.

One of the men shrugged. "I told her to stay inside until we returned."

"And she agreed?" Skye obeying the guards and not hell-bent on helping? As soon as the guards dashed toward the well to draw water, she would be yanking her boots on and following behind.

Panic ripped through Brodie as he dropped the reins and dashed toward the cottage bellowing her name.

Chapter Eighteen

The horse bounced and jolted Skye as they rode swiftly through the dense forest and winding trails. Trees flew by in blurs, and she fought the urge to lash out at the brute behind her, opting instead to spend her energy on figuring out a means of escape, knowing she was no match for her abductors' strength. Ross had pinned her to his chest, but not before she'd been able to drive her fist into his groin.

Luckily, he'd not struck her in retaliation, but had chosen to bind her hands so that she no longer had that option. He'd also stuffed a gag that smelled of sweaty horses into her mouth after she'd bitten a finger of the hand he'd closed over her cries for help.

Afraid the smoke had been coming from Brodie's parents' home, Skye had thrown on her boots and cloak, intending to help with the fire, but had barely left the cottage when Neil grabbed her. Icy dread filled her veins as she stared down Ross, the man she feared would give her over to Argyll and whatever awful fate the Covenanter leader had planned for her.

Swallowing, she said, "Please, I have to help with the fire."

"Nae, lass." Ross climbed onto his horse, and Neil tossed her on after him. "'Tis nothing but a distraction for yer guards. By the time they have it figured out, we'll be long gone."

Ross bolted like the devil himself was after them. And he would be, if Brodie caught up to the arse—he would unleash hell on her abductor. She tamped down her fear, knowing Brodie would come for her. Now, what could she do to slow them down?

But what if he couldn't reach her in time? She'd not even been given the chance to say good-bye to Brodie. Her stomach lurched, and her eyes started to sting. She needed to tell him that if things had been different with all this clan politics and duty, she would have chosen him. Now, if she were able to make it back to her uncle, she would be going to another man's bed, beholden to the MacPherson clan. But her heart would remain at the cottage with Brodie.

"How do ye ken Brodie?" Ross pulled the cloth from her mouth once he seemed to think they'd reached a safe distance from her old home.

Despite her trembling hands and racing heart, the arse would get nothing from her. She held her tongue.

"Skye," Ross intruded again. "Why are ye with Brodie Cameron?"

She was no fool. There was no way she would betray Brodie to a man who held a grievance with him. Brodie had not said much about Ross, but it had been obvious they knew each other, and there was some sort of feud or at least a strained relationship between them.

"Answer me, lass," he commanded as his grip on her tightened. She sensed frustration with her noncompliance, not anger, like he wasn't accustomed to a lass refusing him anything.

"My wrists hurt," she ground out. The pain wasn't unbearable, but maybe if she could convince him to stop, it would give the Cameron men or Brodie a chance to catch up to them. Surely, her absence had been discovered by now.

Silence met her, and she could tell by the decreasing pace, he was contemplating stopping.

"Ye want answers from me? Ye will have to untie me." Surprised at how calm she sounded, she glanced over her shoulder to meet his brooding gray gaze and let him know she was going to stand her ground. She pinned him with steely resolve, even though dread snaked its way through her body and clenched her heart. If he planned to give her to Argyll, now might be her only opportunity for escape.

"Neil, the horses need a break." Ross called to his friend. "But we can't be long."

Coming to a stop, Ross climbed down and drew her from the steed's back. Pulling a knife from his boot, he sliced through the twine, freeing her hands.

Shaking them about, she backed up, keeping her gaze on Ross but trying to watch Neil as well. "How do ye ken my uncle?"

Something akin to fury flashed in his eyes. A shiver ran down her spine, her hands clasping her skirts in hopes of hiding the tremors threatening to give away her fear. Tilting his head to the side, he studied her and instead of answering her question, said, "I admit I am intrigued by ye. I have kenned Brodie a long time, but never seen him so enamored with a lass. There must be something about ye, but he has never mentioned ye." She held her breath as the MacLean circled around her.

"Mayhap that is because there is nothing between us." It hurt to let the words fly from her mouth, because they betrayed her heart, and she knew that no matter where she ended up, despite the lie, she would always have to tell it.

She would always have to deny the secret that she now knew would cripple her.

"Nae, lass. I have spent many nights with Brodie and a bottle of whisky, and no' once did he ever mention ye and those fiery green eyes. That leads me to believe ye mean more to him than just a casual tup."

Her eyes widened, and her mouth fell open. She turned away, but it was too late—he'd seen the anger his words had inflicted. Silence fell over her again. There was no way to respond that would not give away her secret. At least, no way that might not endanger Brodie.

"Yer reluctance to speak of him leads me to believe the same of ye. Does he own yer heart, lass?"

She held her tongue and tried to steer the conversation back to what she hoped was a safe subject as she covertly studied their surroundings, looking for any means of escape.

His gaze caught hers, and he scowled, "We need to be going."

No, she needed more time; she was certain if she got back on that horse her chance at rescue or escape would be gone.

Putting her hands on her hips and staring him down, she asked, "What do ye seek from the MacDonald laird?"

Ross stiffened, and she knew she'd bought a little more time. "He has my father on his island. I need him back, and I need yer uncle's clan to leave my people be." His deep tenor had changed from an easy tone to barely contained rage. Maybe she should be worried about what this man would do to her uncle instead of Brodie, but at the same time, relief set in that he was not going to hand her over to Argyll.

"Ye wish to trade me for yer father?" She recalled what the two of them had said as they had thrown her into that wagon.

"Aye, I do, lass."

"What if he doesnae meet yer terms?" She goaded him,

knowing the distraction was working.

"He willnae let one of his enemies hold his favorite niece."

"Why did he take yer father? I've heard nothing of him." Stepping over to a large rock, she sat and pulled a boot off, inspecting it as if it had a rock in it.

"They're accusing him of murder," Ross scoffed as he paced in front of her.

"Whose murder?"

"Some fisherman."

She inhaled sharply, remembering the journey to Stirling and the incident she'd tried to block out. *Murdina's husband.* "Did he do it?"

"Nae, lass, he had no reason to. My father is a good man, and despite the brutality of yer uncle's clan, we wouldnae attack an innocent man. The MacLeans are better than that." The conviction in his voice was reassuring, but did Ross think the MacDonald clan capable of such cruelty? They were all good, God-fearing men and women.

"Why does my uncle think he did it?" But the name written in sand by the body, his disappearance on their journey to Stirling—he must think the MacLean laird responsible for Niven's horrific death. But that still wouldn't explain him sanctioning attacks on innocent MacLean farmers if he held their laird at Cairntay.

"It doesnae matter. I'm going to get my father back and end the violence before the MacDonald causes a war."

"Do ye no' ken ye may be making things worse by taking me?"

"Nae. I think the MacDonald will agree ye are worth the price of my father and peace."

"Ye will also have my cousins to worry about. Let me speak to my uncle. He will listen to me if I ask him to let the MacLean free." She wasn't certain he would, but if she could show Ross that she held sway over her uncle, maybe she could get away.

"Nae, lass. I cannae take that chance. Put yer boot on. We need to be going." She obeyed because she would need it on when she made a run for the road. They had stayed to a trail by the river, and if the Camerons weren't coming, the well-traveled path to the village might be her only hope of finding someone who could help.

"Ye are only two. Ye are no match for my uncle's men."

He huffed at her response as he started to gather the horses. "Neil will keep ye hidden away until I return with my father."

Too bad Ross was almost likeable, because her uncle and cousins were going to kill him once she was safe.

• • •

Brodie's heart hammered a frantic beat as he raced through the dense forest. He and the guards had been able to find the tracks of two horses and had taken off in pursuit. Once they were sure they had found the right path—following the river north, toward the Isle of Skye—Brodie sent the men for reinforcements. Who had taken her? Was it Ross and Neil? Argyll? He assumed it was Ross, because Argyll's men would have left more destruction in their wake, if not killed Skye as soon as they'd found her.

Damn. The noise he'd heard the night before—it had curdled in his belly and kept sleep from returning, and now he knew why. Instinct had tried to warn him that, despite the extra guards Lachlan had put on the house, they were being watched, but he'd dismissed it.

He should have known better than to let his guard down where Skye was concerned, but his mission as the Royalist Raven had to come first, and she had paid the price for his choices. He had proven yet again that he was unworthy of her, and that being near him posed too many dangers. After all these years, he could still hear the MacDonald's voice ringing in his ears. "He is no' good enough for her."

The pounding of his horse's hooves was drowned by the soft earth and the roaring of the nearby water. The snow had melted, leaving the ground below a thick, soupy mess. Following the river, he was thankful Skye's abductors had stuck to the back way. If the treacherous arses had gone to the main road, their tracks would have mingled with the myriad of others, and it would be harder to find them.

He and Ross had been friends of a sort, making meaningless bets on those drunken nights that had been his sole source of amusement during the first few months of Skye's absence. He continued the friendship despite being the Raven, because the man had always seemed genuine to him.

Now, his companion on those nights, a man who had dark secrets of his own, had his arms wound around her waist. Ross had demons, but Brodie had never thought of the man as dangerous—it was out of character with the fun-loving rogue of a drinking buddy he had been. Whatever his reasons, they would never be good enough to wash away the man's sin of placing a hand on his Skye.

He sharpened his gaze on the path ahead as he imagined Ross riding behind his woman, which sent pulses of rage through his heated blood.

He was going to kill Ross MacLean.

• • •

As laughter reached Brodie's ears, and he realized his quarry had stopped, he slowed his mount, hoping the soft earth and dense trees would mask the thumps of his horse's hoofbeats.

Recognizing Neil's voice, he pulled to a halt. So it was those two arses, after all.

"'Twas luck we left yer family when we did and ran across Brodie in the village."

"Aye, I hated having to go home before tracking the lass down, but it seems to have worked to our advantage."

"I wish I had been able to see his face."

"Enough. I dinnae have a good feeling about this." Ross's reply was quiet and clipped.

Brodie had never heard the man utter anything other than his boisterous, drunken voice or the soft-spoken drawl the rogue used on the lasses. This was the serious, dark man beneath the surface.

After climbing down from his horse, Brodie crept forward, grabbing a large, club-size branch from on the forest floor. He would unsheathe his sword, but he had questions that needed to be answered, and killing the men wasn't currently an option.

"Did she tell ye what she was doing with that Cameron?"

"Nae, she wouldnae. I think she has a soft spot for him."

Brodie studied them through the trees as they gathered their horses, apparently preparing to mount and ride on. Ross's gaze skimmed the trees and almost landed on him, but it kept going, likely watching for his arrival. The man knew he couldn't be far behind, and was probably anxious to put more distance between them.

Skye was safe and sitting on a rock on the other side of the small clearing near the river, facing away from the water and toward the woods as she laced up her boot. Her hair had come loose from the braid she'd twisted it into this morning. She was disheveled and seemed exhausted as she peered into the woods. Not in his direction, so he wouldn't be able to get her attention without alerting the men, but at least she was several paces away from her abductors.

Relief washed over him as he realized she did not appear to be injured. His fists clenched around the club. The bark bit into his palms, but the pain gave him clarity.

Neil came to stand in front of her, just a few feet from his location. "What were ye doing with Brodie Cameron, lass?"

She did not respond.

Neil's face puffed and turned red at her casual dismissal. He stepped closer, "What were ye doing with him, wench?" Spittle flew out of his mouth, and still she did not answer.

Brodie inched forward. That man was not going to lay a hand on his woman.

"Leave her be." Ross's tone had a resigned quality to it.

"We need to ken if he will come after her."

"He will. I saw the way he looked at her. We just have to be on guard and watch for him."

"Then 'tis time we get on our way. This stop has taken too long."

When Neil turned back toward Ross, Brodie lunged.

Chapter Nineteen

A thud reverberated through the air, followed by a whoosh and a lighter thump. Everything went quiet. Even the birds appeared startled. Skye's gaze shot to a form at the edge of the clearing, so familiar her limbs yearned to run to him. At the same time he looked different, distant and hard, like a warrior on the verge of battle. Time froze.

Brodie's muscles were tense and his back bowed as he glared at her captor. Looming over Neil's limp body, Brodie held a stick the size of a small tree trunk. The ice in the gaze he directed at Ross chilled her more than the chill air; small bumps rose on her arms as she pulled them around her midsection in a futile attempt to cocoon her body from the raw anger that was directed at Ross. She was actually frightened for him.

"Whoa, Brodie." Ross's hands were in the air as he backed a step. His gaze darted to the motionless body on the ground and then back to Brodie.

Brodie stayed focused on his prey.

Every muscle in his body was taut and ready to pounce.

She had never seen him so fierce. Even when he'd been furious with his brothers, he had held restraint, but now he looked like a marauding Viking ready to kill. The rage was not directed at her, but she felt the chill of it to her own bones.

"Take one more step toward her, and ye willnae live another day." The menace he directed at Ross made her shiver.

"Hold on, Brodie. Ye ken I would never hurt the lass." He shook his head.

"I dinnae ken what to think of ye anymore. Ye are obviously no' the man I thought ye were." Ross glanced at Skye, but Brodie growled. "Dinnae even look at her." He called over to Skye, "Are ye all right, love?" His tone lightened as he glanced through his lashes at her, but she could tell he was still aware of every move Ross made.

She nodded but couldn't speak. He must have recognized the fear on her face, because his tone eased yet again.

"Come, love." Brodie finally looked directly at her. His gaze softened as he tilted his head to indicate the spot behind him. She rose, but before she could take a step, Ross was between Brodie and her. She was several paces behind Ross, but there was no way around. She gulped and moved slightly to the side so that she could keep watch on both the men.

"I need her. I cannae let ye take her." Ross stood with his hands fisted on his hips.

"Ye wish to die, then?" The words frosted the air like a cold wind.

"If I have to." Ross's frame seemed to double as he squared his shoulders and lowered his balled fists to his sides. He matched Brodie in height, but was slightly broader. "If she means this much to ye, I will return her to ye when I am done with my business."

"Ye have no business with her."

"Ye can have any lass ye want, Brodie. I need this one."

Brodie's grip on the club tightened. He was shaking with barely contained fury. "This is the only one ye cannae have."

"I think we can work this out, old friend." Silence permeated the air, a brief moment of calm before the dam walls broke.

Brodie lunged for Ross with the club, but Ross stooped and hit him in the stomach with his shoulder. The branch went flying out of his grasp as the men connected. They both tumbled to the earth.

Brodie was first to recover. Rolling, he emerged on top of the tangled limbs on the ground and pinned Ross with one arm while he pulled back with his other. Brodie's fist connected with the man's cheek with a heavy thud then slid into the soft soil.

Inching backward, Skye almost tripped over the rock she'd been sitting on. She clasped her hands together, wringing them, as the men continued to pound on each other.

Ross drew his knee into his chest and planted his foot on Brodie's shoulder. "Get off," he grunted as he flexed his leg and pushed with enough force to knock Brodie on his ass. Rolling, Ross came to his feet and braced his legs in a defensive stance with fists ready to strike again.

Her abductor lifted one hand to rub his cheek. "Have ye gone daft, man?"

"Nae, I'm seeing as clear as ever." Brodie stood and faced his foe. They were so intent on each other, it was as if both men had forgotten she was even there.

"I'll take ye out, and we will find ye one even bonnier," he said in a light tone, probably the same one the men used when they were out drinking and wenching together.

"Our drinking days are done." Brodie spit and swung at Ross, who nimbly avoided the swing by ducking to the side.

"Dinnae let a lass come between us, man." Again with the lighthearted tone, but this time it was mingled with disbelief.

It was as if they had some sort of code only men understood, a secret language she'd never been a party to. It seemed Brodie knew it well but was not reciprocating in the fun.

"She is mine."

Skye stiffened at his proclamation. At the same time Ross froze, then his head turned to her with a blank expression.

Brodie pounced and connected with the side of Ross's face.

Ross snarled, more angry than hurt. He swung back, but Brodie evaded the blow. Ross overreached and stumbled, but recovered and came at Brodie again. His fist struck just below the jaw. Brodie inhaled sharply, and his hand rose to finger the tender spot. His gaze returned to Ross's, his eyes cold and dark.

Brodie held back nothing. She honestly thought he would kill Ross, then she looked to the body on the ground, which still hadn't moved. Had he killed Neil with that club?

"And did ye decide she was yers when ye stole her from the back of my wagon?" They moved in circles around each other, and Skye backed to avoid their combative dance. "Why were ye there anyway? There is no way ye kenned what I was doing."

Brodie had never told her why he'd been there the night Ross had abducted her—he had not even known who she was.

"I was trying to find out if ye were behind the raids."

"So, ye are the Raven. I had my suspicions. A member of the Resistance told me the Raven thought I was one of the Covenanters."

"Yer sister?"

"Aye, but she didnae tell me it was you."

The Raven. Skye had heard of the Royalist spy wreaking havoc on the Covenanter's plans to convert all the Catholics in the Highlands by force. But Brodie had not confessed anything to her. Ross had to be wrong.

Or maybe Brodie had been playing her for a fool all along. Could he have used her to get to Ross? Like he'd used her to learn about her uncle?

Skye shook her head to dislodge the words. She wanted to unhear them, erase the truth and pretend he had cared for her and wasn't using her to get information about Ross or her uncle.

The tears fell then, fast and unrelenting. She couldn't stop them, and as the men continued to fight, she gasped at the air that refused to fill her lungs. Struggling to take the next breath, she felt as if she was drowning in pained pride and regret. Stumbling, she tried to yell out, but there was not enough air.

Then she was falling and was submersed in an angry current. She was carried away, drowning in the same river that had stolen her mother.

• • •

A squeak and a flash of movement pulled Brodie's gaze toward the spot where Skye had been standing just moments ago. The space was empty, but for the rock Skye had been resting on. Ross had also stilled and looked that way.

Skye? Where is Skye? Panic engulfed him.

"In the water," shouted Ross.

As the man pointed, Brodie's gaze followed the direction the fingers indicated.

At first there was nothing, then her head bobbed above the current. Fear snaked through his body. Kicking off his boots, he rushed for the edge. His veins turned to ice as he ran for the frigid water. He was vaguely aware of Ross following. "She cannae swim."

He couldn't take his eyes off her or she would be lost.

She was already so far away, and her slight form kept disappearing. Her head dipped above the surface again, and he thought he saw her gasp for breath. She was still in all of her garments. With the bulk the water added to them, they probably weighed more than she did.

Unpinning his plaid, he dropped it and dove out as far as his legs would propel him. Valuable seconds had already ticked away as he'd removed his clothing.

He regretted not persuading her to learn to swim after her mother drowned, but she'd shut him down so fast he never bothered to ask again.

Her protests would not stop him this time. When he got her home, she was going to learn.

When he got her home.

He had to get her home. Her shiny blond locks disappeared again, and his heart gave a painful lurch.

He was closer, but still so far away. The current was strong and relentless, but he used it to propel his body closer, praying he would be in time.

Just a little farther. He was so close to where he'd seen her last. She came up again, but sank so quickly she'd not had time to take a breath, and he kicked harder and dove.

He could see the dark of her plaid billowing under the water and grabbed for it. The heavy, dense material almost slipped through his fingertips, but he was able to grasp it at the last second.

He pulled and was rewarded with the feel of her soft body colliding with his. Wrapping his arms around her malleable form, he pushed up.

When they broke above the surface, she lay limp in his cradling arms. She was pale, head hanging to the side at an awkward angle with flesh that had changed to the temperature of the frigid water, and he couldn't tell if she was breathing.

The plaid draped around her body pulled on something,

dragging them along with the furious current. He couldn't get his footing. If he tried to get it free, he might lose his grip on her.

A splash sounded beside him, and Ross was there. The man's arms steadied him, but whatever had Skye's clothing was stronger than both of them.

"Her plaid is caught. I cannae get it off."

Ross let go of Brodie's shoulders and pulled at Skye's wrap. It did not budge.

Limbs trembling with fatigue as he held on, he kept her head above the water by sheer willpower. If they didn't get her free, he would go down with her, because he was never letting go. If she didn't live, he couldn't.

His eyes blurred as Ross fumbled in the material with no success. The pin that secured the long swath to her unmoving form eluded the man's searching hands. It was lost in the folds of the drenched fabric. Ross grabbed at where it should have been and pulled in opposite directions.

The garment fell from her shoulders, and the weight that was threatening to pull her and Brodie under eased as the material was ripped from around her and carried away with the current. Their accelerated pace down the river slowed.

Load lightened, he kicked toward the shore, careful to keep a firm grasp on the precious bundle in his arms. As the slippery rocks beneath his feet gave way to a thick, sludgy coating of solid ground, he started to run. The oozy mud shifted, and he almost lost his footing but managed to catch his balance just before her head went back under.

Back on shore he collapsed with Skye still in his arms. His gut twisted as the bile in his belly bubbled and threatened to surface. Tilting her head toward his, he tried to speak.

"Skye." The strangled sound was half sob and half command. There was no response.

"Skye." Louder this time.

Connecting his cheek to hers, he was met with ice cold flesh as frigid as the water he had just pulled her from. His ear tilted toward her mouth to listen for any sound of breath.

Nothing.

No. His mind screamed as he rocked her back and forth. *No Skye, Dinnae leave me.*

Despair clawed him, and he pulled her into his chest and squeezed. He willed her to breathe as his shaking hands wrapped her waist. He held onto her as hard as he could, keeping her here and grounded to him.

She convulsed, and a small cough escaped then another and another. His hands flew to her shoulders to hold her up where he could study her face. Her eyes were vacant, but her limp body had stiffened as she continued to cough and sputter. Water dripped from her lips, and with each cough she inhaled sharply. It happened a few more times, then she stilled. Her eyes fluttered and shut, and she collapsed into his chest.

He put his head to her breast and let out a sigh as he heard a slow steady beat and felt the gentle rise and fall of her chest. Relief flooded through him as deep breaths filled her lungs. He said a silent prayer of thanks that she would live.

He didn't know how long he sat there rocking her, but he startled when Ross came up behind him. "Ye need to get her out of the cold."

He didn't look up. "She will be all right." It was more to reassure himself than the man who had risked his own life to help save her. Gathering her closer, he stood with her still cradled in his arms and started in the direction of their cottage.

Raising up a thick colorful bundle, Ross held it out to him. "Dry tartan," the man said.

Nodding, his gaze shifted to focus on the mountain of a man who was standing to the side with the horses—Neil.

Obviously he had recovered from Brodie's blow.

Ross must have seen the doubt. "We have had a talk. Aye, he is still angry and may come at ye later, but he'll wait till the lass is on her feet again."

Brodie gave a curt nod, and Neil did the same.

After covertly divesting Skye of her wet garments and wrapping her ice-cold body in the woolen warmth of two plaids, they climbed up on the horses and set off together toward the house.

"Ye can come back to our place. We have a lot to discuss. 'Tis no' so far, and ye can dry yer clothes," he called to the two men.

"Aye, I'm freezing," Ross said.

The sun was still high above, so they took the main road, since it was faster and there were fewer trees to block its warmth. They had enough time to get home before the dark of the night closed in.

Not wanting to jostle Skye more than needed, he set a slow but steady pace. Some color began to return to her cheeks as she began to warm in his arms beneath the blankets.

Ross cantered up beside him and tilted his head. "How did ye ken she couldnae swim?"

"We have kenned each other since we were bairns." He thought about ending it there, but the man had put himself in harm's way to help save her. "Her mother was lost to the river when she was only eight. She refused to go near the water after that."

"She's the one ye came out to forget all those nights?" Ross's gaze held a silent understanding. The man looked away, and he saw then his old drinking companion had a hidden reason for visiting the tavern as well. He didn't ask—he wasn't sure he wanted to know what demons were beneath the surface, and he was almost certain Ross would not want to share.

"Aye." His tired gaze fell to her. Skye's skin had warmed slightly, and her worried frown had become peaceful and relaxed.

"Ye ken I wouldnae have harmed her?" Ross asked.

He scowled. "I didnae ken what to think. Why?"

"The MacDonald has my father. I need Skye to get him back."

"Ye willnae be using her." He pierced Ross with the intense fury he'd pushed away the moment he saw Skye in the water.

"I am no' a blind man." His old tavern mate's eyebrows rose. "And I dinnae wish to fight ye again." Ross rubbed his cheek.

They rode silently for a while. Ross broke the quiet first. "Do ye ken her uncle? Will he listen to ye?"

Brodie didn't want to squash the hope he heard in Ross's voice, but could not lie, either.

"Nae, the man hates me," he said. "Cairntay is a fortress. Ye will never get to him. Yer best bet is to beg."

"That is the one thing I cannae do." Ross said.

Brodie saw the MacDonald's face sneering at him. The smell of the salty water and the pain in his ribs flashed through his head at the remembered beating by his men.

If he were forced to face the MacDonald again, one of them would not walk away.

Chapter Twenty

Skye realized she was safe in the bed with Brodie. Shuddering, she snuggled closer to his warm body.

"Yer awake, love."

"Aye." Her throat scratched and ached as if the drowning in her nightmares really had torn the breath from her. She'd have to make some tea. "I just had an awful dream."

He sat up and skimmed his hand down her jaw as his brown eyes beckoned with warmth. "Ye are safe here now." The low, sleepy burr of his voice grounded her. "But I willnae ever let ye scare me like that again. When the weather warms, even if I have to come to that awful island, someone will be teaching ye how to swim, and ye willnae have a choice in the matter."

Memories crashed over her just like the punishing currents had, and her breath caught. She had been in the river and had struggled to break through the surface to get to the bank.

"Ye are the Raven?" Shivering, she closed her eyes, not really wanting to know the answer. From all the accounts, he was one of Argyll's most wanted, a dangerous spy capable of sneaking in and out of places undetected and gaining deadly secrets, many of them leading to successful skirmishes against the Covenanter crusaders. Although the Raven's actions were in the best interest of anyone supporting King Charles and the Catholic faith, the brutality and dangers of that kind of lifestyle were unimaginable.

When he didn't reply, she opened her eyes to see him focused on the ceiling. Slowly, he nodded, and her breath caught in her throat. How could he have become mixed up with such dangerous people?

"'Tis why I cannae ask ye to stay." Twisting toward her, he kept her pulled close and continued, "Ye arenae safe with me."

Inhaling sharply, she tried to let all the implications wash over her. "Why?"

"If the Earl of Argyll finds out who I am, he'll go after anyone I care about."

"How did ye get started?"

"I was spying for the old Cameron laird before ye left. 'Tis why I disappeared all the time and couldnae tell ye where I was."

"Ye were spying the whole time."

"When I realized ye were no' coming back, I spiraled down and started drinking and staying out all night. To give me a purpose, Lachlan's father sent me on more missions, but with the ruse of a wastrel. It just kept growing from there."

"The drinking and the wenching?"

"'Twas all a lie. Part of my disguise. No one expects a drunken rogue to be stealing secrets."

He'd not been a lecherous toad, but was a wanted man.

"Were ye no' scared?"

"Nae, at least I had a purpose again."

Her chest felt as if it would cave in—she'd pushed him

into that life. "Ye have to stop."

"I cannae, and 'tis why ye must leave. I've received word yer uncle will be here tomorrow."

The last thing she wanted to do was think about her lonely nights ahead and his spent as a hunted spy. It was too painful and raw to talk about. She just wanted to enjoy this last night with him. Knowing he could not give up his missions to stay with her, she would have to sacrifice him to the Royalist cause. Life suddenly seemed crueler because she was betrothed to another, and according to Parliament, Brodie was a notorious criminal.

Pushing away the pain, she vowed to make the most of their last night, to hold him and make love to him one more time. The memory would have to last her a lifetime because tomorrow, she would have to leave.

His fingers massaged her scalp and sent tingles vibrating through her as her thoughts scattered and his head dipped to gently place his lips on her forehead. The wall she was attempting to resurrect around her heart crumbled a little more.

He shifted up on an elbow; the movement caused her body to slide impossibly close to his. His velvety, tender lips gently touched hers. They were warm and soft, reverent, like he was worshiping her mouth with his. He lingered there, and then his teeth playfully nipped at her lower lip, and a shimmer of desire sparked. It sent needy chills extending into her core, awakening that familiar ache inside her. She arched and moaned.

When he pulled free to gaze down at her, his warm breath was so close she could still taste his honey on her lips.

"That makes me tingle." The words spilled out in a throaty rasp she barely recognized and let him know how affected she was by his touch. Closing the gap between them, he kissed her again, this time with a little more force. When he pulled back, his eyes focused on hers for just a brief moment, and she could have sworn they turned darker.

He claimed her lips, but this time was different. The delicious kiss stole her breath and left her completely at his mercy. The heat of his mouth seared her all the way to her core with each swipe of his tongue. She matched each stroke with her own fevered desire. As their tongues mingled, she thought, *This is heaven.*

Moaning, she reached out for him. Her hand trailed up his taut waist and landed on his ribs, urging him closer. Cherishing the feel of his warm flesh under her palms, she held on to keep herself grounded in this moment, and to let him know she was his and completely lost to the desire coursing inside her.

Brodie's hand fisted in her hair and pulled her closer. She didn't know how it was possible, but the kiss deepened. This man owned her. She had been branded by him, and her heart would never belong to anyone else.

When they broke apart, they gazed at each other. Skye licked her lips as she thirsted for his again. He shifted and kissed her as his arm snaked around her waist to pull her body flush with his. Her sensitive breasts felt hot and swollen against the flesh of his chest.

The caress was slower and more deliberate, as if he had all the time in the world, as if he was intentionally drawing out the moment to savor the taste of her. She didn't mind the leisurely pace. It was pure ecstasy just being in his arms with his lips pressed hers. But that would not be enough as the ache between her legs grew. Her body was ready to feel him plunge inside her tight, slick sheath.

Brodie's lips closed around the most sensitive spot on her neck, the one that always sent waves of need pulsating through her. Her back arched involuntarily, and she felt his long thick shaft hard against her belly. She groaned at the desire to have it buried deep within her.

The ache that was building, and begging for release became a growing desperation. Moisture pooled at her center. His lips followed the curve of her flesh slowly up to her ear.

"Ye are so beautiful, love. I want this to go on forever."

Oh, she did, too, but she also yearned to feel that sweet pressure filling her. Everything outside of this moment ceased to exist; nothing else mattered when she was wrapped in his arms with his body pressed to hers.

His mouth trailed back to the sensitive spot on her neck that screamed for attention. She trembled as his moist heat clenched around her tender skin, and he suckled as he gently moved his head in small circles.

She closed her eyes and tilted her head farther to the side, allowing him full access. She gasped, and his teeth tugged and his lips clasped around the spot as he gently sucked again. A stark primal need raced through her. She could feel herself becoming wetter and knew she was fully ready for him.

The need was urgent now. The desire to have him buried inside her was all-encompassing. She wanted to feel the length of his shaft deep inside her as he drove into her again and again. Her body wanted him. Her heart wanted him.

"Please," escaped from her as she struggled with the need for release.

He pulled back and gazed directly into her soul with a look of desperation, like he was on the verge of losing her. She blinked and looked back at him in confusion.

"Ye are safe now." His hand rose and softly caressed her cheek. It was like he was reassuring himself more than her, then his lips returned to her neck and his hand trailed down her ribs, leaving her skin on fire in its wake. His hot palm landed on her hip and held her.

When he rose up on his knees, the loss of his warmth left her shivering. His gaze fastened on her with such hunger she knew he was walking a thin line on the edge of control.

If she tried, could she send him over that precipice? She was already there, and was on the verge of pushing him to his back and climbing astride him. A wicked smile curved his lips, and his head tilted slightly to the side as if he could read her thoughts.

She expected him to fill her in that moment, to give her body the release it craved. His scorching gaze seared her heart, putting a hot brand there that said *I belong to Brodie Cameron*.

He did not enter her. His head dipped to her breast, and his body slid down hers, igniting fires down her belly and thighs. His hot, searching mouth landed on her breast as his hand sank lower to play in the curls at her apex. Her eyes fluttered back, and her hands clutched at the covers as she surrendered to the feel of his urgent attentions.

When his fingers dipped lower and one skimmed the sensitive nub between her legs, she thought she would cry out at the pleasure.

He briefly stilled, his finger resting on that pressure point that was on the verge of pulling her under the blissful currents about to envelop her. She rotated her hips to urge him to give her that release. He smiled against her chest, and she was afraid he would make her beg.

His mouth covered her breast again and instead of reverent kisses, he took her nipple and the surrounding area into his mouth and sucked, gentle at first, then fevered and urgent. Fire shot through every part of her body. His finger rubbed up and down, over her sensitive nub again and again. It was too much. It was just right. She tried to look down at him and he must have sensed her movement, because his eyes tilted up to watch her with her breast still between his lips.

The climax enveloped her as pleasure rippled from her core outward. Wave after delicious wave assaulted her senses as gasps of undeniable euphoria escaped from her lips. He released her breast and rose slightly, and his eyes devoured her moans of ecstasy. His finger still worked on her apex as the sensations continued to claim her.

Just as the currents started to fade, Brodie removed his fingers and slid back up her body. His chest rose up but his hips impaled hers to the bed. His hard length was poised just outside her entrance. "Ye are so beautiful."

The tip of his cock touched her, and her hips shimmied to coat it in her juices. Despite her release, her body was not done with his. She still craved the pressure of his hard manhood filling her completely.

His warm gaze met hers, and he seemed to struggle with something. "I love ye. I always have," he said, and her heart clenched with happiness and despair.

It was the truth. His soul could not lie to her, so she gave him the truth in return. "I love ye, Brodie Cameron."

He entered her deliberately and painfully slowly. His gaze told her they belonged together, and she recognized the emotion because she felt it also. Her heart almost broke, knowing she would have to go to another and that he could be discovered at any moment.

He started to move, not so much pulling out, but thrusting while grinding his hips into her, reaching her very core. It was as if his body had merged with hers and recognized its home. The primitive dance caused his pelvis to rub against her sensitive nub again, sending renewed waves of urgency flooding through her.

The fullness in her core and the crushing pressure at her center was too much, and a second wave of orgasms, even more intense than the first, rocked through her.

"Brodie," she managed to breath out as her hands reached up to clutch both sides of his head.

His pace increased, becoming fevered and urgent. His

mouth fell open to gasps that matched her own. His eyes glazed over as his hot seed filled her. Her chest swelled, and she soared in the pleasure of knowing that it had been she who had put that look on his face.

He gently sank down on her chest and lay there as his breath slowly returned to normal. Her fingers wove in and out of his thick hair, the silky strands tickling the place where her fingers met. Neither moved. She wanted to remember this, the feeling of sharing their souls.

This night would end too soon, so even when his body slackened into slumber, she was reluctant to slide out from under him. Eventually, the weight became too much, and she maneuvered to the side, leaving his shoulder resting on hers and his arm draped across her belly.

Nestling her head next to his, she caught a whiff of his unique woodsy scent. She would miss that about him, too.

She wanted to cry, but remembered she was supposed to be savoring the night because tomorrow she would leave her heart here with the Raven.

Chapter Twenty-One

"Morning, love." The words were whispered into her ear. Delicious chills spread through her as she stretched awake.

"Umm, 'tis a nice morning." She wrapped her arms around the warm body next to her. Brodie caught her hand, cupped it in his, and brought it to his mouth to place a gentle kiss on the top.

"Sorry to wake ye."

She smiled lazily at him.

"Dinnae look at me like that. We willnae not make it out of here."

"What if I dinnae want to go anywhere?" she asked as she ran her fingers up and down his back.

"We have to get to Kentillie."

Awareness crashed over her.

She forced a smile and pretended it would be easy to leave. "Ye ken he will definitely be there today, then?"

"Aye, Lachlan sent word again late last night."

Their time was over. Now she had to make herself believe she could go back to a life without him.

"How late is it?" She looked to the window, thankful she could peel her burning gaze from his. From the beams shining through the small slit in the curtains the sun had started its ascent into the sky.

"No' too late, but we should eat and get there soon." He gave her a quick peck on her temple and threw the covers back. Jumping up, he retrieved his clothes as if he weren't dying inside like she was. Cold rushed over her, and she shivered.

Brodie had already made her breakfast by the time she'd dressed, and they sat together and reminisced. Just days earlier, she would have thought it heaven, but now she felt it was hell on earth, being unable to savor the moment, knowing they were about to be torn apart.

A knock sounded on the door.

"I'm on my way to the village," came a muffled voice from the other side. Brodie must have recognized the sound because he unlatched the lock then pulled.

Ross. She couldn't think of a logical reason for him to be there, because last time she'd seen him, he and Brodie were fighting.

"Did my parents treat ye right?"

"Aye, 'twas generous of them to let me stay overnight." Ross smiled but avoided looking directly at her.

"I'll send word once the MacDonald arrives." Brodie moved forward to embrace the man as if they were friends. She tilted her head, trying to dislodge her confusion.

"I'll be at the inn or the tavern until I hear from you." The man who should not be there nodded at them. "'Tis good to see ye on yer feet again, lass." Ross smiled at her sheepishly.

She nodded. Was she still dreaming?

Brodie said, "He helped save ye from the currents. We would probably both be dead right now if he hadn't helped." He turned to Ross. "I'll talk to Lachlan about the MacLean and the trouble the MacDonalds are causing on yer land. Hopefully, he'll be able to broker some kind of peace."

MacLean. Skye rolled the name around in her mind. There was something about it. Something she'd seen recently and blocked out.

"'Twill come to war if the man willnae see reason."

"I dinnae think 'twill get that far. Once the MacDonald finds ye helped save Skye, he'll have to let yer father go."

"From what ye tell me, he isnae reasonable. Will he forgive me when he finds I was the reason his niece disappeared from Stirling? And will that stop the MacDonald clan's senseless killings of the MacLeans?"

"My uncle wouldnae attack innocent people. Yer father is the monster," she chimed in, fists balled, angry that everyone kept accusing her uncle of being things he wasn't.

"My father is innocent," Ross countered.

"We'll sort it all out at Kentillie. Where's Neil?" Brodie changed the conversation.

"He went out for a drink last night and never came back. He'll turn up, though. He always does."

"You should go back to the inn. I'll send for ye after I meet with the MacDonald."

Ross nodded and turned to leave.

A short while later, Brodie ushered Skye through the door and walked with her, hand in hand, toward the stable. The sun climbed in the sky on a beautiful but cold day. Although her stomach churned at what she must do, she leaned into his warmth, savoring his scent for the last time. A lump formed in her throat.

Just before they reached the stable, she tightened her grip. "Please, dearest, one last kiss." But even that would not sustain her.

A slow sad smile curved his lips, and his head started to dip towards hers, but his attention was pulled away. She followed his gaze to see a large group approaching from the direction of Kentillie. The riders were too far away to see, but she recognized the unmistakable flag of the MacDonald clan.

Grasping Brodie's arm, she felt more despair than relief. "'Tis my uncle."

He became stiff, as rigid as a tree, and took a step back from her. The cold engulfed her. His expression was stoic and closed off as if he were ready for a fight. And when she looked back to her uncle, fear snaked through her as she recognized her betrothed riding next to him.

A second banner came into view, the flag of her betrothed's family, neighbors to the Camerons. Until now, she'd thought to spare Brodie the news that she'd be living so close, but there was no way to avoid it.

"I need to tell ye before I lose my nerve. That's Collin MacPherson with my uncle. 'Tis the man I'm to wed."

Hands gripped her from behind and yanked her back, away from Brodie, her uncle, and her betrothed.

• • •

Brodie's heart stopped at Skye's admission—his woman would be a married to another man.

Collin MacPherson.

It hit him.

Argyll. He knew the earl was scheming to wed his ally, a Campbell, to the youngest MacPherson: Collin. But with Collin married to Skye, the earl's plan would fall to pieces. That was why he wanted her dead. Her uncle would only propose the match, risking Argyll's wrath, if he was seeking to make a Royalist match.

Her uncle had never been a traitor.

Skye's hand was wrenched from his, and pain erupted from his shoulder. He winced, arching his back. Reaching around, he touched the sensitive spot and pulled his hand away to see crimson dripping from his fingertips.

Scuffling reached his pounding ears and he jerked upright to see Skye struggling with a man who was pulling her toward the dense trees and away from him. Familiar, cold eyes watched him closely as Neil held a knife to Skye's throat. The man he'd clubbed only yesterday glared, eyes bulging with hatred and a hint of madness, reminding him of a rabid dog eyeing a cornered squirrel.

Movement to his right caught his gaze, and he shifted his weight in time to see the surviving bandit who had attacked them days earlier swipe at him with a dirk. Brodie ducked to the side and took up a fighting stance.

"We just want the lass," the bandit said as Neil pulled on Skye's hair to tilt her face up.

"Ye cannae have her." Brodie's claymore was strung over his back; he would lose precious seconds unsheathing it.

The bandit would be no match for him. What concerned him was whether or not the arse had informed Neil that Argyll was offering a reward for Skye, alive or dead.

Brodie launched himself toward the bandit—it was the small one who had trembled like a thistle's seeds blown by the wind, running after their last encounter. Before the man could blink, Brodie had one hand around his neck and another around his wrist, which held the jewel encrusted dirk that had belonged to the bandit's leader. His opponent attempted to break the hold by swiping at Brodie's legs, but only succeeded in losing his own balance.

He fell, and Brodie went down with him. Tangled together, they hit the ground with a thud, and the man's head hit the earth, a whoosh of air escaping from the attacker's lungs. He didn't give the bandit time to recover.

Rising up on his knees, he released the man's neck to strike his face. Bones crunched beneath the blow, and the man squirmed to get out of Brodie's grasp, struggling in vain as Brodie's fist returned again and again to the attacker's face.

Skye screamed, and he turned to see her sprawled on the ground and crawling away from Neil as he drove the knife he'd held up to Skye through the chest of one of Lachlan's guards.

His gaze shifted back to Skye to make sure she was unharmed. She appeared uninjured, but in the time he'd taken to inspect her, Neil had unsheathed a broadsword from his waist. Brodie didn't have time to draw his claymore before the brute charged toward him.

Releasing the limp man, he rolled, but not in time. The blade grazed his arm, and pain exploded at the spot. His hand moved to cover the wound as he continued to roll then bounded to his feet.

Neil hadn't been able to stop his forward momentum, and the traitor's sword pierced the ground. Struggling to pull it from the soft earth, the arse's attention was focused on his indisposed weapon and not him. Neil's sword had landed just shy of the bandit, who came up on all fours and coughed up blood.

Brodie charged before Ross's friend could turn the broadsword on him again. "What are ye doing, Neil?"

"Argyll wants her. The bounty on her head will see my family fed fer years," the brute huffed out.

Catching Neil's arm as the man swung back around, Brodie grabbed the hilt and jerked down, freeing the sword from the mountainous man's grasp. It slipped from his own and fell to the ground.

Struggling for the dominant position, he faltered as Neil's elbow connected with his side. Despite his pain, Brodie was faster and more agile, punching forward into the man's gut. He was rewarded when the bastard folded at the spot of impact and buckled at the knees, falling to the ground.

He kicked at Neil and scored a shot to the man's ribs. Rolling over, the arse writhed on the ground and cradled the spot where the boot had connected.

"Look out," came a shout from Skye. The bandit charged with the dirk in his hand.

Brodie was too slow, and the knife pierced his side. Blinding pain seared through him. The man pulled the dirk back and plunged toward him again, but this time, Brodie caught the bandit's hand and twisted until the knife fell from his opponent's grasp.

Punching with his other hand, his fist collided with the man's scrawny face, and the bandit crumbled to the ground. While stooping to pick up the dirk, Brodie heard the angry grunt of a threat headed his way.

Neil was on him again. Just as the traitor reached him, Brodie sank the blade of the dirk into soft flesh of his opponent, and Neil stilled. Twisting the blade, he pushed deeper. Blood bubbled from the man's mouth before he went limp and slumped onto Brodie's shoulder.

Pushing the body off, he kept his grip on the knife as the man crumpled lifeless to the ground. The bandit still writhed on the ground. Brodie held his hand pressed to his side and sighed with relief when he saw Alan standing over the man, an angry glare in his eyes.

Neither man would threaten Skye again.

Excruciating pain radiated from his wound and blood oozed from the sliced skin. Swaying, he dropped to his knees then fell back on his ass. He blinked a couple of times, then gentle hands pulled at his plaid to get at the injury.

"Sit back. Let me look at the damage." Skye was leaning over him.

"Let the healers deal with him." The MacDonald's voice permeated the fog.

"Nae, he needs me."

Aye, she was right, he needed her. Clarity took hold, and he knew he couldn't go back to a life without her. He could no longer be the Raven. If he had to, he'd take her somewhere far away where they could be safe, but they would be together.

"This is nae place for a lass. I have to get ye out of here now," the stern laird argued.

If he lived through this mess, he would find a way to prove to that arse he was worthy of her. He would dig himself out of the tangled world of deceit and danger that his life had become.

Skye was the only thing that mattered.

"Nae, Uncle, I love him. I'm staying with him until we can get him to Maggie."

"Nae, Skye. Yer uncle is right. Let him protect ye," he huffed out before darkness enveloped him.

Chapter Twenty-Two

Slumping sideways on the bench at a corner table, Brodie swirled a caramel colored ale around his cup and studiously avoided the gazes of the other tavern patrons. The brew smelled of malted yeast and earth. It appeared surprising smooth, with a pleasant scent, but he didn't lift the glass to his mouth.

Skye was gone.

He'd not been able to see her before she had left Kentillie, and he could only just now sit astride his horse without the wound in his side knifing him with pain.

Several lasses in the tavern attempted to catch his eye, but he glanced away every time they approached. He even had to give some a gentle nudge from his table. He didn't want company, and if all went according to plan, he was about to break free from the facade he'd kept up for years, anyway.

The last time Skye had left, he'd drowned himself in ale and lasses. It had never helped, and this time he didn't even want to try. The feel of her skin on his was still too fresh to let it go. Her lavender scent clung to blankets, the furniture, and every crevice of the house. He needed the memories because it meant she had been his again.

The day after the altercation, he'd woken in the room where Maggie treated the ill, then developed a fever and hadn't been coherent or capable of moving from the bed for another three days. By the time he was lucid, the MacDonald and Skye were gone. Maggie had kept his movements so restricted he'd not even been able to warn the arse that the betrothal to Collin he'd made for Skye put her life in jeopardy.

Robbie appeared once his fever had broken. The lad had been so secretive and apprehensive since his arrival at Kentillie that they had barely spoken. He went straight into his reason for the visit. "I was in the village getting herbs for Maggie when I overheard Neil MacLean tell that Covenanter he kenned where the girl was. I rushed to tell Lachlan. I'm sorry I didn't know where you lived, or I would have gone to you first."

He nodded, giving the boy a smile. "Och, 'tis all right. Ye did what ye could."

Robbie thrummed his finger back and forth over what looked like a cross he kept hidden beneath his shirt. Sighing, the lad raised his blue gaze to meet Brodie's. "There is more."

"Just tell me." Placing his hand over his side, he straightened and attempted to sit up on the bed, the wound pulling and making him wince.

"I heard the MacLean man tell the Covenanter that you were the Raven."

Oh, hell. "Did he tell anyone else?"

"I don't know for sure, but he seemed quite friendly with some other men in the village I didn't recognize."

"Thanks for letting me ken," he said as the boy turned to go without another word.

Despite Brodie knowing he could never be with Skye and keep her safe, thoughts of her with Collin MacPherson ate at him. They had lost so much, but he could no longer sit back.

It was time to fight for the life—and the woman—he'd always wanted.

Meeting with Lachlan, Malcolm, and Alan behind closed doors, he told them of the plan he'd devised while recovering. His laird gave him the title of Ambassador of the Cameron Clan, affording him a secure position with little risk. Better yet, when he needed to make occasional trips, he could take Skye with him, or she could stay at the castle so she wasn't alone.

They agreed with his scheme, Lachlan saying, "'Tis time ye had yer life back," and he could have sworn even Alan approved.

Now, he was playing his part one last time and hoping to shed his roguish image before the day was done. Alexander Gordon was the key—if he were to make a clean break, he would need the rebel leader's assistance.

The chair behind him scraped across the floor, and he glanced over his shoulder to see Alex Gordon's dark, amused eyes. "Ye dinnae look so good."

"I feel even better." He would have laughed, but it hurt too much. "I need a favor."

"Well, what is it?" The man sat and Brodie feigned attention to the brew in his hand.

"I'm getting out." He was met with silence. "There is a body near the tall oak by the well on the other end of the village."

"Why should I care?" Alex's deep voice held a hint of interest.

"I need yer help."

Silence again.

"I need ye to turn it over to Argyll's men and claim it's the Raven. The man was at many of the taverns when I stole secrets. 'Twill be believable. Take the reward. Do what ye want with it, but I need ye to forget who I am." He hoped the man had some compassion and would help him out of a life that would get them killed.

"Why should I?"

"It will steer suspicion away from ye. How could they think ye a Royalist sympathizer when you've delivered one of their most wanted?"

"I'll do it. What's his name?"

"Neil MacLean." His shoulders relaxed and released the tension that had been coiling in his chest.

"Ye are sure this is what ye want?"

There was no doubt in his mind this was what he had to do. "Aye. I've been given a second chance."

"Well, take it, and we'll never meet like this again." It almost sounded like admiration in Alex's deep unyielding tone.

"Thank ye," he would miss these clandestine meetings, but he had better plans for the rest of his life, if it was not too late to stop a wedding. "And, one last thing. Get Isobel out. Someone kens who she is. She needs an alibi and to be far from yer group next time there is an attack."

"Ye ken how stubborn she is, but I'll try."

"Stay safe." He pushed his chair back, knocked over his ale one more time for posterity, and stumbled out of his life as the Raven.

• • •

Brodie had just finished packing supplies for the journey to the MacDonald stronghold when a fist hammered on his door.

Ross stormed in. "I'm going with ye."

"I kenned ye would. 'Tis why I told ye to meet me here." Reaching into the bag he'd found hidden in his stables upon returning from his sick bed at Kentillie, he pulled out what he wanted Ross to see and tossed it on the table for his inspection.

"'Twas the bandit's. He survived and admitted this bag

was his."

"'Tis the MacDonald flag." Ross shrugged and let the flag fall back to the table.

"He said they'd been exiled by the Earl of Argyll and told if they could start a feud between some of the Royalist clans, he would welcome them back to the Campbell clan. They were trying to start a feud between the MacDonalds, the Camerons, and the MacLeans."

"Why?" Curiosity piqued, hope burned in Ross's eyes. It was a feeling Brodie knew all too well at the moment.

"They have been raiding our land and cattle, burning our farmers' homes, killing families, and raping our women." The conversation he'd overheard outside the door at the inn where he and Skye had stayed came back to him.

Stuffing the flag back in the bag, he drew out another. Holding it up, he displayed a Cameron flag, then he did the same with a MacLean flag.

"They framed yer father." The attacks on the Cameron land were the reason Brodie had sought out Ross and followed him to Stirling to begin with. It appeared Argyll and his bandits were behind it all.

Ross let out a long breath. "Does the MacDonald ken?"

"Nae. We didnae find it all until after he'd left."

"If he sees this, he may let my father go before my clan gets there."

"What are ye talking about?"

"My brothers. They are gathering an army to invade the Isle of Skye as we speak, but we can beat them if we hurry."

"Aye, I just left Kentillie and told Lachlan we were going. I'm leaving now." He looked at Ross. "Are ye ready?" The man nodded.

"I'm sorry about Neil. I didnae ken he would do something like that. Seems that bandit met him in the bar the night ye hit him with the tree branch. He was looking for revenge against ye, and for the money."

"'Tis done. Let's go while we have light."

Skye was worth it, worth fighting for. Steeling himself for the journey to that damned island to retrieve her, he knew this time he wouldn't beg, he would fight. And he wouldn't leave until he had her in his arms or he was dead.

• • •

Skye studied the boats gliding across the calm waters below her window as the sun's midday reflection shone back up at her. She'd been back at Cairntay for days now, a painfully torturous counting of minutes as she waited for her uncle to return. Tapping her foot, she tried to be patient until the vessels sailed close enough for her to run down and catch him.

Giving her no chance to explain back at Kentillie, he'd taken her in a fierce embrace and then promptly sent her ahead with some of his men while he stayed behind to consult with Lachlan. As soon as she'd been off Cameron lands, she'd wanted nothing more than to turn around and go back, but her uncle's men had orders to get her to Skye safely and, despite her pleading, wouldn't take her back.

After stopping at an inn the first night, she'd spent the whole time crying and feeling sorry for herself, and for Brodie, because she'd not even had the chance to say good-bye. Her heart ached at leaving him wounded after he'd tried to save her from the bandit and Neil. She had no idea if he'd lived or died.

The second night, at another inn, she'd been so lonely and despairing, she'd slunk down to the common room and ordered whisky, despite disapproving glares from the MacDonald men. If she'd stayed up in that cold, empty room alone she'd have gone mad.

As she drank, the room started to blur, and a comfortable

numbness washed over her. She understood why Brodie had turned to drink when she'd left without explanation, why he had sought solace in taverns and then the life of a spy. And she'd left him again.

She beckoned to her soon-to-be betrothed, who had been traveling with them and sat a few tables away. He had kept a respectable distance from her, possibly under her uncle's orders. At her invitation, Collin MacPherson rose, swaggered forward, and eased into the chair across from her.

"'Tis glad I am to see ye happier, lass. Those bonny green eyes shouldnae ken sadness, but drinking it away willnae help."

"What will?" She honestly wanted to know what could make the pain go away.

"Facing yer troubles."

"Huh." She was already facing one of them. "Do ye really wish to marry me?"

"I wanted to court ye to see how we would do together."

Comprehension dawned. He wanted more from a wife than a woman to warm his bed—he was looking for love. In Stirling, he had been giving her a way out of the arrangement if they did not find each other mutually agreeable.

"I have already given my heart to another." Burying her head in her hands, her eyes stung as the despair returned.

"Brodie Cameron."

She peeked up at the mention of his name.

"Aye." Her gaze drifted to the ring she still wore on her finger. Reverently, she touched it to her lips.

"He is a lucky man."

"'Tis the other way around."

"From what I have heard, the man isnae worthy of yer affections." Collin's voice had an edge to it.

"'Tis all my fault."

"Nae, lass." Collin said gently. "I release ye from the

arrangement."

Panic set in. What would happen to the alliance with her uncle's clan? She just shook her head.

The fear must have been evident on her face because he continued, "I will tell my father that 'tis my doing. Our alliance will be safe."

Hope bloomed in her chest. "Ye are certain?"

"Aye. After yer uncle returns and we are able to discuss it, I plan to go back to meet with the Cameron laird." Collin rubbed the back of his neck.

Suddenly feeling exhausted, she yawned. "'Tis time I retire." She banged her thigh and rattled the table in her haste to retreat.

"Good night, Skye," he called. She could feel his eyes boring into her back as she fled up the stairs.

Not even knowing if Brodie lived, she cursed herself for the millionth time for not forcing the subject with her uncle so she could stay in Kentillie. She prayed he would honor her wishes, and it wouldn't be too late to get back.

Not caring if Brodie lived as a spy, or about the danger it put her in, she needed to be with him. It would probably mean many nights of loneliness waiting for him to come home, but he was worth it. She could handle the nights alone if she knew he wouldn't desert her.

Last time, she'd sat back and waited for Brodie to come get her, but now she was willing to fight for him. Her home was with Brodie in the little cottage where she'd grown up. Of course, the hard part would be convincing him to let her stay.

Upon her arrival at Cairntay, she'd walked into the kitchens and had seen Murdina's sullen face. Scattered bits of memories dislodged and fell into place like the stars lighting up the heavens.

The words etched in the shore by Murdina's husband were like the ones spelled out by the murdered MacLeans, just enough to incriminate other clans. Then, she remembered where she'd seen the knife with the amber hilt the leader of the bandits had held—it had belonged to Niven, Murdina's husband.

The MacLean laird had done nothing wrong. Her uncle had put Ross's father in the dungeon for another man's crime.

Skye paced as she waited for her uncle's boat to get closer. A smaller boat she could barely see had pushed off after them, but she concentrated on the larger one. When it reached the halfway mark, she rushed from her room.

As she reached the shoreline, her uncle disembarked. Pulling to a stop in front of him, she rested to catch her breath. She almost coughed as a cool breeze laced with the scent of mist and fresh water filled her lungs.

"Is Brodie all right?"

"He lives. Ye have some explaining to do, lass."

Relief flooded through her. Ignoring his words, she continued, "The MacLean laird is innocent."

His eyes narrowed on her. "What do ye ken of the MacLean?"

"He didnae kill Murdina's husband. The bandits Brodie fought did it."

"Nae. Niven wrote the laird's name before he died."

"Ye are wrong, Uncle. The bandit wrote it after Murdina's husband was dead. He had Niven's knife. I kenned the first time I saw it something was wrong, but I couldn't remember where I'd seen it. Niven had often helped Murdina in the kitchens, and I remembered the amber jewel in the hilt. There is no' another like it."

"'Tis no' enough to say he didnae do it."

"I have to go back." She grabbed onto his arms and pleaded.

"Back where?"

"To Kentillie. To Brodie."

"Ye just got home." Her uncle's gaze sharpened, and he

studied her intently, as if some epiphany had been revealed and snapped into place. She could have sworn he was smiling with approval, but his lips didn't turn up. Had something changed his opinion of Brodie?

"I need to see Brodie. I have to tell him."

Shouts rang out.

The little boat had just made it to the shore and two men disembarked. A familiar figure strode purposely toward her uncle and her. Relief washed over her as her eyes took in the healthy glow of his skin. Brodie was all right.

Her heart lighted, the weight of the last few days lifted, and for the first time since leaving Cameron lands, she felt like she could breathe.

Brodie didn't look at her; his gaze was fixed instead on her uncle.

What appeared to be delight flashed in her uncle's eyes as he seemed to grow larger. Surely she was mistaken, unless he was happy about destroying the man who had pursued her again.

"Angus, get Skye up to Cairntay. She doesnae need to see this."

Angus grabbed her by the arm and pulled her toward the path up to the castle. Trying to pull away was no use because his firm grip kept her pinned to his side. But, she hadn't yet told her uncle she didn't want to marry Collin MacPherson and that he'd agreed to seek out a Royalist match with the Camerons. She needed him to know she wouldn't be happy unless she was with Brodie.

No one here knew how much she loved him and wanted to be with him.

Shivering, she recalled what her uncle had done the last time Brodie came for her.

They were going to kill him.

Chapter Twenty-Three

"'Tis the MacDonald."

Brodie's gaze followed Ross's tilt of the head but didn't make it past the slim form whose back was turned toward him.

He didn't need to see her face. It was Skye, with her long hair billowing in the wind, as her beautiful hands flew through the air to make some point while Alastair MacDonald looked on.

After leaping over the side of the boat, he strode toward them.

Ross called out, "Guard yer left side. That wound is no' yet healed." He said something else, but the words didn't register.

Brodie still had doubts whether Skye would leave with him or if he could convince the MacDonald that he was worthy of her affections, but life wouldn't be worth living without her.

Whether she wanted to be with him was irrelevant at this point. He had to get her off this island. An army of MacLean men was headed this way, and if the MacDonald didn't hand over their laird, a war was about to take place.

And he had to let the MacDonald know of the danger his proposed marriage to the MacPherson clan posed. Surely, he would dissolve the agreement when he learned Argyll would stop at nothing to seal alliances with the other clan, ensuring they sided with the Covenanters in the ongoing battle for loyalties.

The MacDonald's gaze landed on him. Brodie gritted his teeth.

Show no fear.

The laird said something to the man beside him without taking his eyes from Brodie, and Skye's figure disappeared down the shoreline.

Squaring his shoulders, he strode to within arm's length and pinned the laird with a determined gaze.

"I have come for Skye. I want her as my wife."

"Ye are too late. She is already betrothed," Alastair MacDonald answered.

Collin MacPherson appeared at the MacDonald's side and glared at him. He'd not been on the boat with the rest of the disembarking MacDonald men and had just joined the group.

"Nae. 'Twould be a mistake. She belongs with me, and the marriage puts her in danger."

The laird's headed tilted, so Brodie plowed forward, "The Earl of Argyll willnae allow a Royalist match with the MacPhersons." Sparing a glance toward Collin, whose jaw tightened, he continued, "He wishes to wed a Campbell to this one. He thinks 'twill get the MacPherson laird to swear loyalty to the Covenanters. He offered a reward for Skye's death or capture as soon as she was gone from Stirling."

"My father would do no such thing," Collin protested, but Brodie thought he could hear a drop of doubt.

Alastair MacDonald's gaze drifted from his for the first

time, taking dark and deadly aim on the MacPherson man, then calming and returning to meet his unwavering stare. "What if she doesnae wish to go with ye?"

"Let me speak with her, and she can tell ye herself."

"Did ye no learn from last time?"

Fifteen or so of the MacDonald's men stood nearby, and he would face them all if need be. Despite their number, he would fight until he couldn't. He braced for the beating that was sure to come.

"Aye, I did learn. I didnae fight hard enough." The MacDonald's lip curled up slightly as something almost like approval danced in his eyes.

"Then show me ye are the right man to keep her safe." The laird nodded to the man at his side. "Collin, I think 'twill be between the two of ye. After all, ye have also come a long way to seek her hand."

"Uncle." He thought he heard Skye's voice carry in the wind.

Collin stepped closer as the other men backed away then made a show of taking the claymore from his back and throwing it to the ground. Brodie did the same.

The man took up a fighting stance with fists raised just below chest level, and he was assailed with a sense of calm he'd not expected when it dawned on him—the man wasn't intent on Skye as his prize. If he were, he would have held on to that sword, because she was a bounty worth dying for.

Matching Collin's position, he pulled his shoulders back and felt the stretch of skin where the wound in his side had been stitched.

"I dinnae like to see a lass cry."

Skye. Why is she crying?

Bam, Collin's fist hit his cheek and Brodie's body twisted with the motion. Shaking his head, he returned to the fighting position that so far had proven to be useless.

"Ye dishonor my clan with yer accusation."

Och, 'tis the real reason the man is angry.

Collin lunged for his midsection and they both flew backwards. Air rushed from his lungs as they landed on the stony beach. He pivoted and was able to shake the brute.

The man dove at him again, but this time Brodie lifted his foot and caught Collin in the chest. Pushing out, his opponent fell back on his ass.

The brute scrambled to his feet, but so had Brodie, and he drove his fist into Collin's face. Wincing as his knuckles collided with bone, a sharp pain assailed his hand with a sickening crunch. He shook it out.

Collin looked dazed, but threw another punch. He caught his opponent's forearm and threw his other hand into the man's cheek. Collin pulled him flush and then pushed out. Losing his grip on the man's arm, Brodie stumbled.

The man's fist sailed through the air, and Brodie easily dodged down and out of range. The brute threw another that he also also deflected. He swung, and Collin ducked in time to miss the blow.

"My father is nae Covenanter." Steel hardened in the man's voice. He charged again and they tumbled to the ground once more. Rolling over, Brodie jumped up first, but his side felt as if the stitches in it had ripped his skin apart.

Collin stood and was met with Brodie's fist. The blow to the temple was wide and off its intended mark, but still the man looked dazed and fought to keep his footing.

"Stop!" Skye's voice broke into his haze.

Brodie turned to see her running toward them.

"Ye arenae worthy of her," Collin said. His next punch landed on Brodie's left side. Dizziness enveloped him and he fought to keep his footing as his hand went to cover his injury.

Nae, he was good enough.

Inhaling sharply, he tried to catch his breath as the world

started to spin. His hand felt warm and wet and he glanced down to see it covered in blood. Falling to his knees, he clutched at his side, fighting back the wave of nausea that assailed him, and struggled to his feet.

"Nae, Collin. Stop." Skye's voice broke through the wall of fog and suddenly, she stood between them.

Backing to him, she held out her arms in a protective stance. He tried to block out the sweet scent of her and the warmth that enveloped him at the light touch of her skirt swishing against his legs.

He gently took her by the shoulders and moved to the front of her, shielding her from Collin. "Move away, love. I dinnae want ye to get hurt."

His gaze returned to Collin's face where he thought he detected something like approval. Confused, he took a deep breath and out of the corner of his eye, saw a satisfied smirk on the laird's face.

"Nae, Brodie. 'Twill be all right. This is my fault." She laid her hand on his arm and smiled up at him. She looked at The MacDonald. "I wish to return with Brodie. I love him, Uncle. And Collin and I have spoken about it. He willnae hold my decision against the clan." Her palm slid down Brodie's arm and took his hand in hers.

His heart thumped out of his chest.

"All these years we have been separated because of a misunderstanding, and because I wasnae brave enough to seek out the answers I needed. 'Twas nothing Brodie did. 'Twas me and my stubborn pride."

Her gaze returned to him and she squeezed his hand, warm and reassuring.

"I love Brodie. I want nothing more than to be with him the rest of my life." His heart swelled and overran with sheer joy. "If he will have me." Her teeth tugged at her bottom lip and he wanted desperately to put his mouth on hers, but some sense of preservation won out, thinking he should wait for her uncle's approval before giving in, in front of the MacDonald's men.

He lowered his temple to rest on hers. "Aye, love. I wouldnae have come to this godforsaken place if I didnae want ye." He tried to laugh but the movement pulled at his wound and it came out as a shudder.

"Aye. 'Tis time ye both came to yer senses." The MacDonald stepped forward and clasped him on the shoulder, causing him to stumble. Brodie's other hand came up to steady himself on Skye's arm.

She gasped. "Yer hurt."

"Nae, 'twill be all right. I just need to sit a moment."

Anger flashed in her steely green eyes as she pierced the MacDonald, then Collin. "Look what ye have done. Ye kenned he was injured."

"Angus, help the Cameron lad up to Cairntay so we can have someone look at it."

"He is nae a lad anymore and 'twill be my husband. Ye can call him Brodie."

Did she just scold the MacDonald?

Men moved in to lift him under the shoulders, but he didn't want to let go of Skye's arm. Squeezing her hand, he shook his head.

"'Tis all right, Brodie." Her hand brushed his cheek. "I promise, 'twill never leave yer side again."

• • •

Skye bounded up the steep stone steps much lighter than when she'd come down. Her uncle was beside her, but she kept her gaze pinned on Brodie's back. Her heart sang louder than the seagulls swooping near the shore as she took in the broad expanse of his shoulders and the way he tried not to lean on her uncle's men.

He came for me.

"Skye." A familiar voice burst into her thoughts.

"Ross. Ye came with Brodie?"

"Aye. I'm sorry about Neil. I didnae ken he would do something so desperate." The remorse in his tone was genuine, so she nodded.

Turning her gaze back to Brodie, she asked, "How bad is his side?"

"'Tis no' so bad. He probably just ripped the stitches." Ross looked at her uncle, and she remembered why he must be here.

"Uncle, 'tis someone ye need to meet," she said as they reached the summit of the long stone steps that led up to her uncle's castle, Cairntay.

"I am Ross MacLean, son to the MacLean. I am here to see my father freed."

Her uncle's eye's darkened. "Ye are the same MacLean who kidnapped my niece." The menace that dripped from his voice was thicker than the heaviest mist she'd ever seen on the beach below. There was a reason men feared her uncle; he could be ruthless when crossed.

"He helped save my life, Uncle."

"Ye wouldnae have been in trouble if it hadnae been for him."

"I wouldnae have found Brodie again, either."

He nodded then returned his stare to Ross. "The MacLean murdered a man in cold blood." Anger dripped from each word.

"Nae, 'twas no' my father. 'Twas the bandits who were trying to take Skye to Argyll. They had these." Ross opened his pack and pulled out wads of material. He held out the cloth for inspection.

Angus stepped forward. "'Tis the MacDonald flag and a MacLean and Cameron in here as well." He held one open for her uncle to see.

"Ye found these on the bandit who took Skye?"

"Aye. Brodie did. The one he beat lives and confessed to all the raids and the murder of yer man."

"'Twas who had Niven's dirk." Skye put her hand on her uncle's arm and noticed he had paled. He was probably thinking of how he'd held the MacLean laird without cause for almost three weeks.

"Ye will want to release him before my brothers get here with an army of MacLeans. They willnae be far behind me."

Her uncle gave a slight nod. "Inside for some food and ale. I'll have yer father join us."

"I'm going to see to Brodie." Knowing Ross would be safe in her uncle's care, Skye smiled, wiggled around her uncle, and took off in a sprint to reach him. They'd made it so far she had almost lost sight of him. The men guided him through the doors of a stone building near the castle just as she arrived back at his side.

Warmth and the scent of strong whisky washed over her as she entered the small one room building. Her throat was tight and she pulled at the sudden weight of her clothes.

Since she'd arrived back at Skye, she'd been surrounded by a cold misty shroud she couldn't shake. It had melted once she'd seen Brodie on the beach.

A wall lined with beds was empty but for one reclined man coughing in the cot farthest from the door. A graying woman sat by the fire. Setting her knitting down on a small table, she rose and pointed to an empty bed several away from the sick man.

After he lay down, the motherly woman inspected his wound in silence. Brodie recoiled as she poked at it.

Skye maneuvered to the other side of the bed and took his hand as fear returned at the sight of how pale he'd become. Pulling his cool hand to her lips, she savored the feel of his skin. He tasted of salt and wind.

The door swung open. "Skye, once ye are done in here, both of ye come and find me."

She pulled back but didn't let go. "Aye, Uncle," she called as she peeked toward the door.

Her gaze returned to see Brodie's fixed on her. It was warm and hopeful. The door banged shut. His finger traced the ring she still wore. "Ye didnae throw it away."

"Nae. I havenae taken it from my finger."

He let out a long breath then flinched when the woman working at his side poked him.

"Are ye all right?"

"I am now."

"'Tis no' much I can do for it." The woman put her hands on her hips and looked at Skye instead of Brodie. Her heart dropped. "I will re-stitch it, but 'twill be up to ye to keep it clean and take care of him after that."

"He will be all right?"

"Aye. Just needs time to heal properly. No sudden movements. He should stay in bed and keep still for a few days." The woman studied her then Brodie. "Keep yer bed play gentle, too."

Brodie laughed then groaned. Her cheeks heated and she pulled on her plaid at the suddenly warm room.

"Lean him up a bit and give him this." The cup the healer passed her was filled with an amber liquid that made her nose twitch. The oak scent almost burned her nostrils. He'd feel nothing if he drank that.

"I'll get my supplies." The woman walked back toward cabinets near the door.

They still held hands but she reached with her other to run her fingers through his hair. "I didnae want to leave ye. My uncle sent me back before I could talk to him. I'm so sorry."

"Why did ye no' tell me ye were betrothed to Collin

MacPherson earlier?"

"Why did it matter whom I was to wed? Ye never once told me ye wanted me to stay, then I found out ye were the Raven."

"Argyll wants ye dead because he wishes to make an alliance with the MacPhersons. He wishes to change the MacPherson loyalties by marrying one of his cousins to Collin."

It made sense the attacks started the day after her betrothal to Collin had been arranged.

"That should no longer be a problem, because I intend to spend the rest of my life with ye. And dinnae argue with me. If ye have to continue on with yer work, I'll stand by ye and take the risks that come along with it. I dinnae want to be alone, but being without ye is worse."

"The Raven is dead. No one will come looking for him. Marry me. There has never been anyone for me but ye, love."

Elation sweeping in and carving out all the worry and doubt, she leaned into him and nestled her head into his chest. "I love ye, Brodie Cameron." Tears threatened to fall with sheer joy.

"I love ye, too, stubborn lass." Pulling back, his hands rested on her cheeks and his gaze met hers. "Promise me ye willnae leave me again."

"I promise."

His head tilted to hers and their lips touched. Gently, he ran them back and forth over hers in a tender caress that left her feeling loved. She closed her eyes and savored the sensation of Brodie on her lips, knowing she would always want more.

"Hey now, ye two. Lay back down and let me finish."

. . .

A little later, they walked hand in hand into her uncle's solar. Ross paced in front of the blazing fire as her uncle sat stony faced and brooding in his chair. There was no sign of the MacLean.

Skye said to her uncle, "I wish to marry Brodie before he realizes I'm a fool."

"Ye arenae a fool."

"Aye, I have been. Will ye send for the priest and give us yer blessing?"

"I already have."

"Ye have to let Collin ken the Earl of Argyll is willing to murder anyone who stands in the way of him creating an alliance with the MacPhersons. 'Tis why he tried to have me killed."

The MacLean strode into the room, his gaze flying toward Ross. Pride glowed in the matching stormy gray depths.

"'Twould seem the Earl of Argyll was trying to pit us against each other," her uncle started.

They sat around a table while Ross and Skye filled the others in on the truth of the plot. Her uncle's face showed little emotion as they recounted the tales.

"So it seems my men are on their way here. I am assuming ye dinnae wish to go to war with us and please Argyll?"

Her uncle nodded. "Aye, I would like to make things right, and the last thing I wish to do is please that arse."

"Then I suggest we form an alliance."

The MacDonald's eyes narrowed but he said nothing, because he had wrongfully imprisoned the MacLean. What could he say without starting a war?

"Yer oldest son is unmarried."

"Aye."

Skye didn't like where this was going and she was sure her uncle wouldn't either, but some sort of recompense was called for.

"My daughter is in need of a husband." The MacLean's gaze pierced her uncle's.

"Father. Isobel will—" Ross objected but his father cut him off with a quick, "psst," then he looked back to her uncle.

"Do ye agree?"

Outrage, then resignation flashed in her uncle's eyes. "Aye. 'Twill bring our clans together."

Skye wanted to protest. She'd overheard Neil and Ross discussing his sister and knew she was far from the gentle sweet maiden that her cousin would prefer to replace the docile wife he'd lost shortly after his marriage. As her uncle had no choice, she bit her tongue.

"Then 'tis time I be getting back to my people before they attack yers. I'll send word with arrangements after they have been made." The MacLean stood and turned toward Ross.

"The wedding will be here." Ross's father froze then turned back at her uncle's words.

For a moment it looked as if the MacLean would object, but her uncle continued, "My son will one day be the MacDonald. He will marry on the Isle of Skye in front of his clan."

A few tense moments passed as the MacLean stood silent. "Aye, 'twill do." Turning toward the door again, he called over his shoulder, "Ross, how do we get out of here?"

"Angus, get the MacLean's horse and see them safely across to the other shore," her uncle commanded the man who was standing just outside the door.

The MacLean nodded and strode from the room, apparently having had enough of her uncle's hospitality. Ross nodded at them and followed his father from the room.

After they had disappeared into the hall, her uncle's steady gaze turned to her and Brodie, who had come up to stand beside her.

"Ye wish to marry?"

"Aye, Uncle. I told ye." She took Brodie's hand and entwined her fingers with his.

"Ye are a man now and not the child who came to take

her the first time. Do ye swear to love and protect her with everything in ye?"

"Her happiness and safety are all I want." Brodie's hold tightened on her hand.

"Then to the chapel. The priest is ready, but ye will be staying here until ye are healed, and I'll have a group get ye home when 'tis time. And no more spying. Yer first duty is to my niece now."

Brodie paused and she exchanged a knowing glance with him. Guessing that Lachlan must have told her uncle Brodie's secret, she now understood the amusement that had shown in his eyes on the beach.

Brodie nodded to her uncle and somehow kept the smile from his face. His dimples peeked through his impassive gaze, and she suppressed the urge to giggle like a little lass herself.

Returning her uncle's gaze, she asked, "Can I have a few moments alone with Brodie first?"

He nodded and pushed back, "Dinnae keep me waiting long. I may change my mind."

"Aye."

He marched from the room. When the door clicked closed, still holding his hand, she asked, "Is this what ye want Brodie?"

"Have ye gone daft, love? 'Tis the only thing I've ever wanted." His free hand came up to caress her cheek.

"Even if it means ye will never have a bairn?"

"I told ye I would be happy just to have ye."

"I am so sorry that I didnae come to ye. That we lost all these years."

"Shh, love, 'tis done. What is in front of us is all that matters now. Will I be enough for ye?"

"Ye are the only thing that will ever be enough for me. I love ye."

"I love ye, too."

Epilogue

Brodie kicked the snow from his boots on the doorframe as he stepped over the threshold. The smell of cooking meat and fresh bread drifted through the air, making his belly rumble as he moved across the room to his own slice of heaven. The only good that had come from Skye's years with her uncle was this amazing talent she had developed in the kitchen.

He spent many a night eating dinner with extra mouths at the table and only sometimes felt guilty over kicking people out of their home to be alone with his wife.

Raghnall met him with whimpers and a nonstop wagging tale. The dog just barely reached his knees, but some nights it greeted him with acrobatic jumps that had him questioning whether the dog was part bird. Raghnall's happy eyes didn't leave its master as he ran circles around him, proudly showing off a bone Skye must have given him. It protruded from one side of its mouth as the dog kept a firm grip on the coveted prize.

It bumped into a chair, and Skye's cat hissed at the disruption to its bathing routine. He didn't know what she saw in that fluffy, big-eyed creature from hell, but he didn't care. The happiness in his wife's eyes when she sat with it cuddled in her lap made the little rat with fur worth keeping around.

Skye rounded the corner with Darach on her hip. His heart soared at the sight of their babe in her arms. As the wee lad had grown in her belly, he'd been afraid of losing her or the babe, but it had been an easy pregnancy and birth.

A boy with blond curls and green eyes that matched hers. They had named him after her father.

"There ye are." She bounced over and gave him a quick kiss on the lips and shivered.

"Ye are so cold."

"Ye will have to warm me, love." He liked the blush his teasing always brought to her cheeks.

"Nora brought some venison from Tormod. How was yer day?"

Smiling, he reflected on the ease with which Skye and Nora had settled into a friendly relationship, even sometimes planning excursions together. "'Twas a long day, but I'm happy to be home."

"Can ye take Darach? I would put him down, but he keeps walking into the kitchen, and I dinnae want him near the fire."

"Aye."

She waited while he bent over to take his boots off and place them by the door. "Sit. I'll bring in the food."

He strolled over to the table as Darach gripped his finger. "Did ye take care of yer mother today?"

She whirled back into the room. "He kept me running around everywhere is what he did today."

Setting down a tray of meat and potatoes, she then eased into the chair opposite to join them. He helped himself and she cut into a pastry he hadn't noticed on the table. She put a large slice on her own plate. "Ye made a tart?"

"Aye, would ye like a slice?" She didn't wait for him to answer, but piled a large piece on a plate and slid it toward him.

"Ye havenae made one of these in a while."

He took a bite as he bounced Darach on his knee. The sweet filling hit his tongue and his senses sparked. He froze and managed to finish chewing before he swallowed. "'Tis raspberry."

She gave him a sideways grin, and her bonny eyes lit with mischief. "Aye, Maggie has found some way to grow them this time of year."

He inspected it with his fork and steaming red berries with a cream mixture seeped from the flaky pastry. "'Tis what ye always wanted when ye had this one in yer belly."

His heart sang as his eyes rose to the prettiest smile he'd ever seen.

Acknowledgments

Special thanks to:

Robin Haseltine, my editor, for her continued faith in me and all the hard work and time she has dedicated to making the Highland Pride series the best it can be.

Jessica Watterson, my amazing agent, for being my advocate and sounding board. I'm truly blessed to have found you.

My best friend, my husband, for his love, support, and for understanding when I get that far off look in my eyes and lose track of our conversation as stories come to life in my head.

My kids, for encouraging me and being proud of what I do.

Jen, Kellen, Amy, and Kelli for our friendship as we stay fit and enjoy life together.

My writing tribe, for sharing their enthusiasm, love of the craft, and wisdom along with keeping me motivated and on track. I will always be eternally grateful to: Harper Kincaid, Denny S. Bryce, Jennifer McKeone, Robyn Neeley, Nadine Monaco, Eliza Knight, Madeline Martin, and everyone in WRWDC.

And for you, the reader who picked up this book and gave me a chance to share a piece of my heart.

About the Author

Lori Ann Bailey is a winner of the National Readers' Choice Award and Holt Medallion for Best First Book and Best Historical. She has a romantic soul and believes the best in everyone. Sappy commercials and proud mommy moments make her cry.

She sobs uncontrollably and feels emotionally drained when reading sad books, so she started reading romance for the Happily Ever Afters. She was hooked.

Then, the characters and scenes running around in her head as she attempted to sleep at night begged to be let out. Looking back now, her favorite class in high school was the one where a professor pulled a desk to the center of the room and told her to write two paragraphs about it and the college English class taught by a redheaded Birkenstock-wearing girl, not much older than she, who introduced her to Jack Kerouac. After working in business and years spent as a stay-at-home mom she has found something in addition to her family to be passionate about: her books.

When not writing, Lori enjoys time with her real life hero and four kids or spending time walking or drinking wine with her friends.

Visit Lori at www.loriannbailey.com. Or, follow her on Facebook at https://www.facebook.com/Lori.Ann.Bailey.author

Discover the **Highland Pride** *series…*

Discover more Amara titles...

LADY EVELYN'S HIGHLAND PROTECTOR
a *Highland Hearts* novel by Tara Kingston

Playing bodyguard is not in Gerard MacMasters's plan but Lady Evelyn Hunt is in danger, and it's up to him to keep her alive. After a crushing betrayal at the altar, Evelyn wants nothing to do with love. Kissing a gorgeous rogue is one thing, but surrendering her heart is another. When she stumbles upon a mysterious crime, nothing prepares her for the dashing Highlander who may be her hero—or her undoing.

THE MAIDEN'S DEFENDER
a *Ladies of Scotland* novel by E. Elizabeth Watson

Madeline Crawford is a daughter of the disgraced Sheriff of Ayr. Fierce Highlander Teàrlach MacGregor was her father's head guardsman. They dream of a future together. Those dreams come to naught when Madeline is betrothed to the son of her warden. Madeline and Teàrlach's love is forbidden but Teàrlach vows to fight, even the king, to make her his.

Tying the Scot
a *Highlanders of Balforss* novel by Jennifer Trethewey

At first, Alex Sinclair, the future Laird of Balforss, has difficulty convincing Lucy FitzHarris to go through with their arranged marriage. Once Lucy arrives, she cannot resist the allure of her handsome Highland fiancé. But when Alex betrays Lucy, she is tricked into running away. Alex must rein in his temper to rescue his lady from unforeseen danger and Lucy must swallow her pride if she hopes to wed the Highlander she has come to love.

The Lady and Mr. Jones
a *Spy in the Ton* novel by Alyssa Alexander

Jones, born in the rookeries, was saved as a young boy and trained to be an elite spy. He serves His Majesty in espionage, hunting rogue spies. Cat Ashdown is a baroness. She knows every detail of every estate that commands the largest income in Britain—yet her father placed her inheritance in trust to her uncle who is forcing her to marry against her will. The baroness's battle against law and convention leads her to Jones and results that are surprising...and possibly unwanted.